D0661710

Lagos Noir

Lagos Noir

edited by Chris Abani

BROOKLYN, NEW YORK, USA
BALLYDEHOB, CO. CORK, IRELAND

This collection is comprised of works of fiction. All names, characters, places, and incidents are the product of the authors' imaginations. Any resemblance to real events or persons, living or dead, is entirely coincidental.

The introduction to this volume was adapted from "Lagos: A Pilgrimage in 13 Nations" by Chris Abani *(Farafina,* 2007). "Showlogo" by Nnedi Okorafor first appeared in an earlier form in *Fantasy for Good: A Charitable Anthology* (Nightscape Press, 2014).

Published by Akashic Books
©2018 Akashic Books

Series concept by Tim McLoughlin and Johnny Temple
Lagos map by Sohrab Habibion

ISBN: 978-1-61775-523-1
Library of Congress Control Number: 2017956557
All rights reserved

First printing

Akashic Books
Brooklyn, New York, USA
Ballydehob, Co. Cork, Ireland
Twitter: @AkashicBooks
Facebook: AkashicBooks
E-mail: info@akashicbooks.com
Website: www.akashicbooks.com

ALSO IN THE AKASHIC NOIR SERIES

ATLANTA NOIR, edited by TAYARI JONES
BALTIMORE NOIR, edited by LAURA LIPPMAN
BARCELONA NOIR (SPAIN), edited by ADRIANA V. LÓPEZ & CARMEN OSPINA
BEIRUT NOIR (LEBANON), edited by IMAN HUMAYDAN
BELFAST NOIR (NORTHERN IRELAND), edited by ADRIAN McKINTY & STUART NEVILLE
BOSTON NOIR, edited by DENNIS LEHANE
BOSTON NOIR 2: THE CLASSICS, edited by DENNIS LEHANE, JAIME CLARKE & MARY COTTON
BRONX NOIR, edited by S.J. ROZAN
BROOKLYN NOIR, edited by TIM McLOUGHLIN
BROOKLYN NOIR 2: THE CLASSICS, edited by TIM McLOUGHLIN
BROOKLYN NOIR 3: NOTHING BUT THE TRUTH, edited by TIM McLOUGHLIN & THOMAS ADCOCK
BRUSSELS NOIR (BELGIUM), edited by MICHEL DUFRANNE
BUENOS AIRES NOIR (ARGENTINA), edited by ERNESTO MALLO
BUFFALO NOIR, edited by ED PARK & BRIGID HUGHES
CAPE COD NOIR, edited by DAVID L. ULIN
CHICAGO NOIR, edited by NEAL POLLACK
CHICAGO NOIR: THE CLASSICS, edited by JOE MENO
COPENHAGEN NOIR (DENMARK), edited by BO TAO MICHAËLIS
DALLAS NOIR, edited by DAVID HALE SMITH
D.C. NOIR, edited by GEORGE PELECANOS
D.C. NOIR 2: THE CLASSICS, edited by GEORGE PELECANOS
DELHI NOIR (INDIA), edited by HIRSH SAWHNEY
DETROIT NOIR, edited by E.J. OLSEN & JOHN C. HOCKING
DUBLIN NOIR (IRELAND), edited by KEN BRUEN
HAITI NOIR, edited by EDWIDGE DANTICAT
HAITI NOIR 2: THE CLASSICS, edited by EDWIDGE DANTICAT
HAVANA NOIR (CUBA), edited by ACHY OBEJAS
HELSINKI NOIR (FINLAND), edited by JAMES THOMPSON
INDIAN COUNTRY NOIR, edited by SARAH CORTEZ & LIZ MARTÍNEZ
ISTANBUL NOIR (TURKEY), edited by MUSTAFA ZIYALAN & AMY SPANGLER
KANSAS CITY NOIR, edited by STEVE PAUL
KINGSTON NOIR (JAMAICA), edited by COLIN CHANNER
LAS VEGAS NOIR, edited by JARRET KEENE & TODD JAMES PIERCE
LONDON NOIR (ENGLAND), edited by CATHI UNSWORTH
LONE STAR NOIR, edited by BOBBY BYRD & JOHNNY BYRD
LONG ISLAND NOIR, edited by KAYLIE JONES
LOS ANGELES NOIR, edited by DENISE HAMILTON
LOS ANGELES NOIR 2: THE CLASSICS, edited by DENISE HAMILTON
MANHATTAN NOIR, edited by LAWRENCE BLOCK
MANHATTAN NOIR 2: THE CLASSICS, edited by LAWRENCE BLOCK
MANILA NOIR (PHILIPPINES), edited by JESSICA HAGEDORN
MARSEILLE NOIR (FRANCE), edited by CÉDRIC FABRE
MEMPHIS NOIR, edited by LAUREEN P. CANTWELL & LEONARD GILL
MEXICO CITY NOIR (MEXICO), edited by PACO I. TAIBO II
MIAMI NOIR, edited by LES STANDIFORD
MISSISSIPPI NOIR, edited by TOM FRANKLIN
MONTANA NOIR, edited by JAMES GRADY & KEIR GRAFF
MONTREAL NOIR (CANADA), edited by JOHN McFETRIDGE & JACQUES FILIPPI
MOSCOW NOIR (RUSSIA), edited by NATALIA SMIRNOVA & JULIA GOUMEN
MUMBAI NOIR (INDIA), edited by ALTAF TYREWALA
NEW HAVEN NOIR, edited by AMY BLOOM
NEW JERSEY NOIR, edited by JOYCE CAROL OATES
NEW ORLEANS NOIR, edited by JULIE SMITH

NEW ORLEANS NOIR: THE CLASSICS, edited by JULIE SMITH
OAKLAND NOIR, edited by JERRY THOMPSON & EDDIE MULLER
ORANGE COUNTY NOIR, edited by GARY PHILLIPS
PARIS NOIR (FRANCE), edited by AURÉLIEN MASSON
PHILADELPHIA NOIR, edited by CARLIN ROMANO
PHOENIX NOIR, edited by PATRICK MILLIKIN
PITTSBURGH NOIR, edited by KATHLEEN GEORGE
PORTLAND NOIR, edited by KEVIN SAMPSELL
PRAGUE NOIR (CZECH REPUBLIC), edited by PAVEL MANDYS
PRISON NOIR, edited by JOYCE CAROL OATES
PROVIDENCE NOIR, edited by ANN HOOD
QUEENS NOIR, edited by ROBERT KNIGHTLY
RICHMOND NOIR, edited by ANDREW BLOSSOM, BRIAN CASTLEBERRY & TOM DE HAVEN
RIO NOIR (BRAZIL), edited by TONY BELLOTTO
ROME NOIR (ITALY), edited by CHIARA STANGALINO & MAXIM JAKUBOWSKI
SAN DIEGO NOIR, edited by MARYELIZABETH HART
SAN FRANCISCO NOIR, edited by PETER MARAVELIS
SAN FRANCISCO NOIR 2: THE CLASSICS, edited by PETER MARAVELIS
SAN JUAN NOIR (PUERTO RICO), edited by MAYRA SANTOS-FEBRES
SANTA CRUZ NOIR, edited by SUSIE BRIGHT
SÃO PAULO NOIR (BRAZIL), edited by TONY BELLOTTO
SEATTLE NOIR, edited by CURT COLBERT
SINGAPORE NOIR, edited by CHERYL LU-LIEN TAN
STATEN ISLAND NOIR, edited by PATRICIA SMITH
ST. LOUIS NOIR, edited by SCOTT PHILLIPS
STOCKHOLM NOIR (SWEDEN), edited by NATHAN LARSON & CARL-MICHAEL EDENBORG
ST. PETERSBURG NOIR (RUSSIA), edited by NATALIA SMIRNOVA & JULIA GOUMEN
TEHRAN NOIR (IRAN), edited by SALAR ABDOH
TEL AVIV NOIR (ISRAEL), edited by ETGAR KERET & ASSAF GAVRON
TORONTO NOIR (CANADA), edited by JANINE ARMIN & NATHANIEL G. MOORE
TRINIDAD NOIR (TRINIDAD & TOBAGO), edited by LISA ALLEN-AGOSTINI & JEANNE MASON
TRINIDAD NOIR: THE CLASSICS (TRINIDAD & TOBAGO), edited by EARL LOVELACE & ROBERT ANTONI
TWIN CITIES NOIR, edited by JULIE SCHAPER & STEVEN HORWITZ
USA NOIR, edited by JOHNNY TEMPLE
VENICE NOIR (ITALY), edited by MAXIM JAKUBOWSKI
WALL STREET NOIR, edited by PETER SPIEGELMAN
ZAGREB NOIR (CROATIA), edited by IVAN SRŠEN

FORTHCOMING

ACCRA NOIR (GHANA), edited by NANA-AMA DANQUAH
ADDIS ABABA NOIR (ETHIOPIA), edited by MAAZA MENGISTE
AMSTERDAM NOIR (HOLLAND), edited by RENÉ APPEL & JOSH PACHTER
BAGHDAD NOIR (IRAQ), edited by SAMUEL SHIMON
BERLIN NOIR (GERMANY), edited by THOMAS WÖERTCHE
BOGOTÁ NOIR (COLOMBIA), edited by ANDREA MONTEJO
COLUMBUS NOIR, edited by ANDREW WELSH-HUGGINS
HONG KONG NOIR, edited by JASON Y. NG & SUSAN BLUMBERG-KASON
HOUSTON NOIR, edited by GWENDOLYN ZEPEDA
JERUSALEM NOIR, edited by DROR MISHANI
MARRAKECH NOIR (MOROCCO), edited by YASSIN ADNAN
MILWAUKEE NOIR, edited by TIM HENNESSY
NAIROBI NOIR (KENYA), edited by PETER KIMANI
SANTA FE NOIR, edited by ARIEL GORE
SYDNEY NOIR (AUSTRALIA), edited by JOHN DALE
VANCOUVER NOIR (CANADA), edited by SAM WIEBE

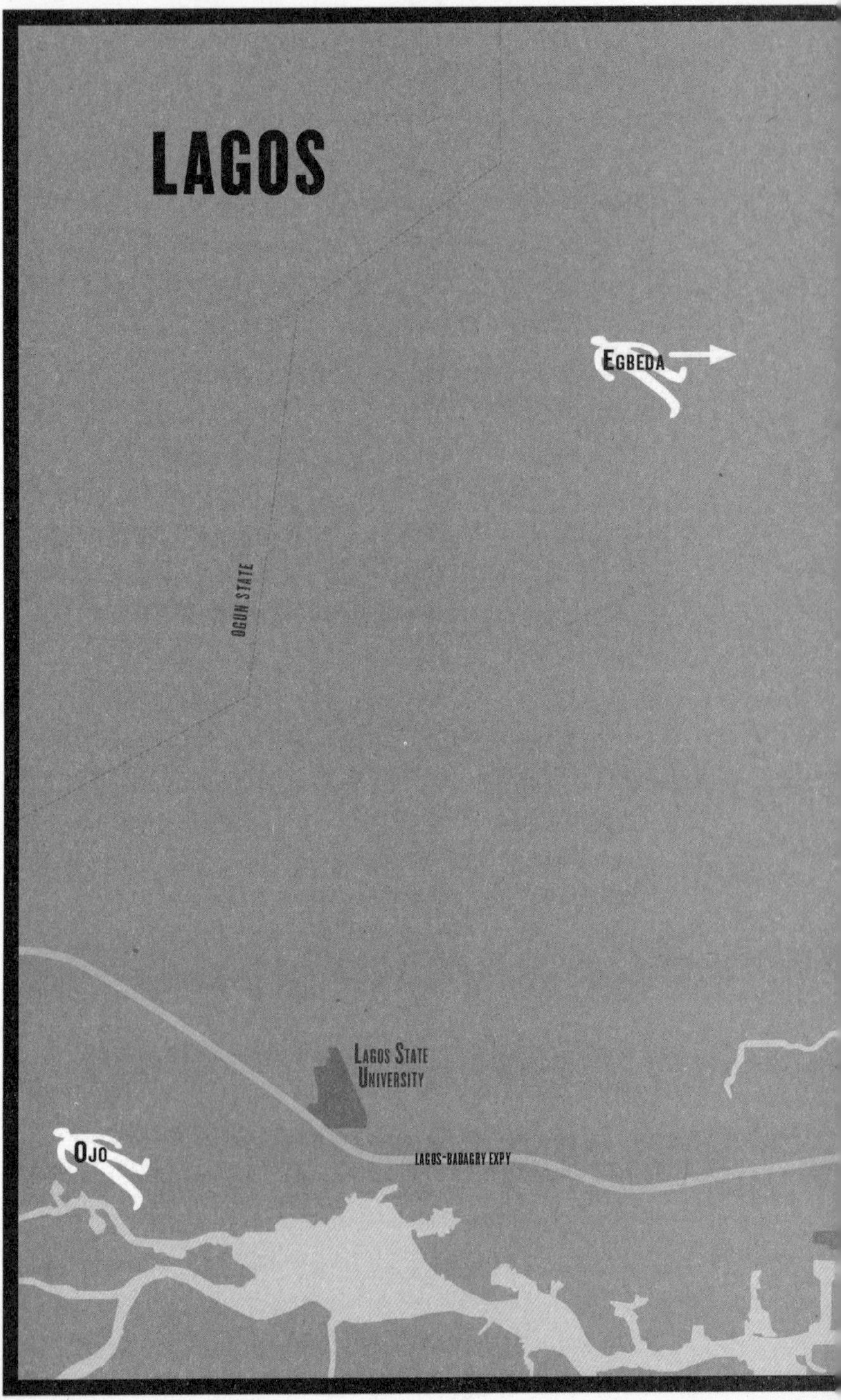

LAGOS

EGBEDA

OGUN STATE

LAGOS STATE UNIVERSITY

OJO

LAGOS-BADAGRY EXPY

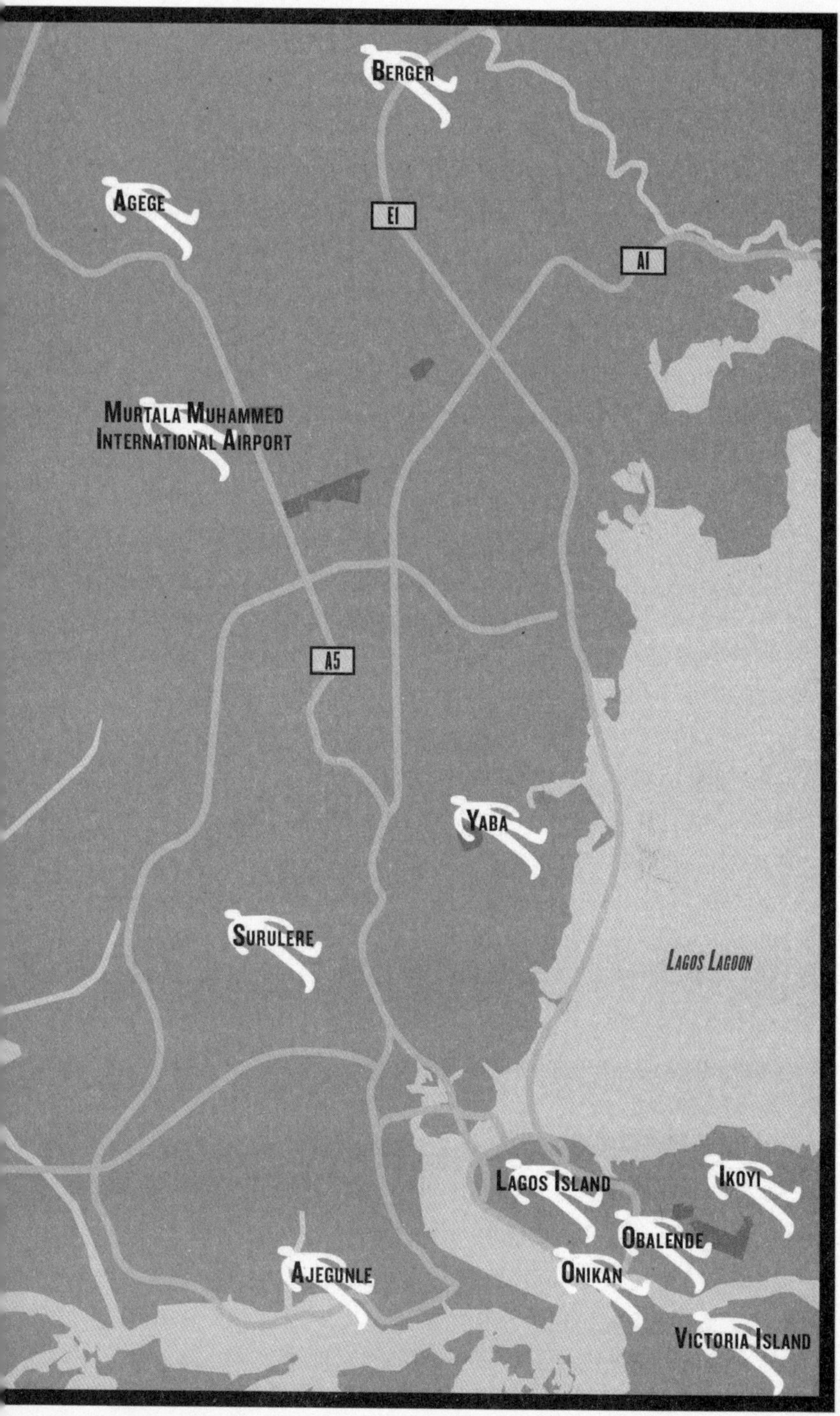

Berger

Agege

E1

A1

Murtala Muhammed
International Airport

A5

Yaba

Surulere

Lagos Lagoon

Lagos Island

Ikoyi

Obalende

Onikan

Ajegunle

Victoria Island

Table of Contents

PART III: ARRIVALS & DEPARTURES

INTRODUCTION

Lagos Never Sleeps

I am listening to Lagos with my eyes closed.

My first memory of Lagos is one I cannot trust. I was four, maybe five years old and my family, my mother and my four siblings, have just returned from London where we fled in 1968, as the war in Nigeria raged for its second year.

Ikeja Airport in 1970 has few amenities to offer us, particularly since my mother has been a vocal pro-Biafra activist in England during the Nigerian-Biafran civil war, one of the many war wives who spoke up against the British government's support of the Nigerian side. We were held for questioning in a hot tin-roofed hangar for hours. This is only what I remember.

An okra and palm oil stew that nearly burned my lips off is my second memory of Lagos. It was 1980 and my mother, my sister, and I were heading back to London. We were on our way to Lagos by car because the flight we were supposed to take from Enugu to Lagos had been cancelled—and then rebooked at twice the price to other passengers. So, my brother had accompanied us by road and after an eight-hour trip in a nauseously hot taxi, we had stopped in Shagamu, fifty miles outside of Lagos, for a roadside café lunch. Even then, Lagos had sprawled out to Shagamu.

* * *

My third memory of Lagos is about my Uncle William. I didn't know I had an Uncle William until he died when I was fifteen. Two men appeared on our doorstep claiming to come from my Uncle William's congregation. It turns out that having failed out of school in Germany and having not returned to the village for my grandmother's funeral, William was exiled not just from the family, but also from the memory of the family. And yet he haunted it, from his small Santeria-based church in the worst ghetto of the city, Maroko.

It was in search of this uncle, this memory, this loss that I couldn't even shape my tongue around, that I went to Lagos for the first time as an adult: hitchhiking alternately by train and lorry; a stupid but exhilarating journey. It was in Maroko that I found the Lagos inside me.

Lagos has, like many coastal cities, a very checkered and noir past. It is the largest city in Nigeria and its former capital. It is also the largest megacity on the African continent, with a population approximating twenty-one million, and by itself is the fourth-largest economy in Africa. Though named by the Portuguese (*Lagos* means *lakes* in Portuguese; the city was also known briefly as Onim) because of the many islands and lagoons that make up its sprawl (it has since had so much land reclaimed from the city for its expansion that it bears no resemblance to that time), its pronunciation, with its subsequent British history, has been anglicized. Surest way to annoy a Lagosian is to call it by its Portuguese pronunciation.

It was previously inhabited by the Awori and then it was under the rule of the Benin Empire, then the British, and then independence. It was known locally as Eko, then Onim, then Lagos, then in slang as Lasgidi, and gidi, and on—the city of many names that wears as many faces as there are people.

People from Lagos call themselves Omo-Eko, children of Eko. It is a beautiful, chaotic, glorious, resplendent, mess of a city. In many ways Eko makes New York feel like a small town.

The Yoruba, who are the natives of Lagos, have lived in urban-style locales for over seven thousand years, some of the earliest people to do so. Cities by their very nature lend themselves to noir, or at least the earlier antecedents of noir—morality plays and, one can argue, even the Penny Dreadfuls of Victorian London. But classic noir as we have come to know it is an invention of the post–World War II era, an invention that is used to express the ennui and desperation that followed the two wars.

The horrors of the slave trade and the subsequent colonial expansions of empires into Africa did much to shake the European sense of moral superiority. But it was something about the nineteenth century, the Victorian obsession with death perhaps, that really ignited the fire for noir. There was Jack the Ripper, the work of Arthur Conan Doyle, and then Joseph Conrad. Conrad's *Heart of Darkness* was written after his visit to the Belgian Congo. What happened there, the horrors the Belgians perpetrated against the Africans—amputations for not paying taxes, amputations on children to compel obedience among adults—is old history now. But then, it was happening. A sympathetic reading could be that this evil inherent in whiteness was too much for a mind like Conrad's, so deeply mired in the myth of white moral superiority to accept, so he projected outward the darkness onto the Africans, making them less than human, as though that somehow justified what was going on. The First and Second World Wars did the rest, shredded what was left, and the noir genre was born. It ranged from hard-boiled detective fiction to more general suspense, thriller, etc.

Nigerians fought in both the First and Second World Wars on behalf of the British. The men who served lived through hell and came back to no pensions and no job prospects. But the struggle for independence was the focus of the elite, and so not much attention was paid to the returning soldiers, and to the feelings of emptiness and horror that they must have shared with their European counterparts. The literature that bears the closest resemblance to noir were the pamphlets of the Onitsha Market pulp varieties.

It is rumored that there are more canals in this Lagos than in Venice. Except in Lagos they are often unintentional. Gutters that have become waterways and lagoons fenced in by stilt homes or full of logs for a timber industry most of us don't know exists. All of it skated by canoes as slick as any dragonfly. There are currently no moonlight or other gondola rides available.

Christ Church Cathedral rises from the slump of land between the freeway and the sea and Balogun Market, like Monet's study of Rouen Cathedral. In the shadow, in the motor park that hugs its façade, is the best "mama-put" food in Lagos. Its legend travels all the way across the country. The seasoned Lagosian gastronomes can be heard chanting their orders, haggling with the madam—*Make sure you put plenty kpomo*, or, *No miss dat shaki. No, no, no, dat other one*. There can be no sweeter music, no better choir. In the distance, bus conductors call like Vikings from the prows of their ships, testing the fog of exhaust fumes—*Obalande straight! Yaba no enter!*

In the shadow of high-rises, behind the international money of Broad Street, the real Lagos spreads out like a mat of rusting rooftops.

* * *

In Ikoyi Bay, boats dot the sea, sails like lazy gulls catching the breeze. Across the bay, the millionaires' village that was once Maroko sits in a slight mist. I think it is the ghost of that lost place haunting the rich to distraction, so that even their twelve-foot walls, barbed razor wire or broken glass crowning them, or the searchlights, or the armed guards, cannot make their peace with the moans of a woman crying for a child crushed by the wheels of bulldozers. Or maybe it is just the wind sighing through palm fronds.

Like in any world city, there are so few original inhabitants that they wear their Eko badges like honor. There is nothing like Bar Beach on a Sunday afternoon. The sand is white, the diamond-shaped all-glass Union Bank Building across the street reflects the water and makes you think it is a wave frozen in time. Children ride flea-infested horses, squealing in a childish delight that is a mix of fear and awe. Slow-roasting lamb suya blankets everything with desire. A cold Coca-Cola here tastes like everything the ads on TV promise—I shit you not.

In one corner, as though they stepped out of a Wole Soyinka play, a gaggle of white-garbed members of the Order of the Cherubim and Seraphim church dip themselves in the water, invoking the Virgin Mary and Yemoja in one breath.

Gleaming cars—BMWs, Lexuses—line the waterfront, spilling young people giddy with money and power and privilege and sunshine.

All of this belies the executions that used to happen here in the 1970s. Families gathered to cheer the firecracker shots from the firing squads dispensing with convicted robbers.

* * *

But as with much of the world, none of it exists until we arrive and cast our gaze about. And so, it wasn't until the early seventies that I realized Lagos even existed as a place. My introduction was detention in a hot military aviation shed where my mother (and thus us), on our return to Nigeria after the Biafran War, was held for interrogation for being a Biafran supporter.

Those of us who grew up in the detritus of the war knew, and many of us still know, and carry, an unsettled darkness. A danger, a sense of the ominous we cannot explain. There was death around us, as memory, as suffering, as a scent that permeated everything we did. Even our play was marked by that war; unexploded grenades that went off as we played catch with them, skulls still in helmets, bullets everywhere, burned-out armored cars. And then the guilt of the war—collaborators who were killed, publicly sometimes or privately. Then there were the suicides, people who couldn't live with who they were and who hung themselves. And then the aunties who couldn't stop crying, grieving for what had been lost in the war, either men or their innocence. That stays with a person, becomes a second skin you forget you are wearing.

But my first real intimation of Lagos and noir was *Lagos Weekend*, a Saturday publication, a newspaper I wasn't meant to read. It was like the *National Enquirer* and *True Crime* had merged. There were salacious stories of affairs, of marriages broken down, of women driven to murder their husbands by a jealous rage or for fear of being beaten to death. Men with penises cut off by angry wives. Murders, burnings, lynch mobs—many of the stories were followed by gritty photographs that were hard to make out but that didn't censor mutilated bodies and other dark subjects, none of them suitable for a child. But I would steal my father's copy, hide behind the water tank, next to the sugarcane clump, ignoring the vampires my brother convinced me lived in them, and I would devour the paper, the cheap ink sticking to my fingers and palms, leaving a residue, a darkness.

The seventies were also a period of the photo novel, a magazine that was like a TV episode or a short film. A story played out in panels with writing and stark black-and-white photographs, a storyboard, but more. They were amazing, and had titles like *True Africa*, and *Monster of Doom*, and *She*, and *SuperMask*, and *Rex Bullit*, and *Chunkie*—they were either costumed superheroes, private detectives, maverick cowboys, or mystical women. But the most popular was a detective called Lance Spearman. Lance wore neat suits, shiny shoes, smoked cigarettes, sported a mustache and a porkpie hat, looking like a low-rent Richard Roundtree in *Shaft*, and I loved him. I wanted to be Lance Spearman. Lance took on all kinds of criminals and won, even an African Blackbeard serial killer. Published by *African Film Magazine* and *Drum Magazine*, these photo books were noir at its best. Many of them came from Kenya, Zimbabwe (or Rhodesia, as it was still known in those days), South Africa, and also Nigeria.

The complex network of spaghetti bridges that make up the Berger-built freeways limns Lagos like the cosmopolitan city that it is. Driving at night across them, you end up on Third Mainland Bridge and the dazzle of lights on the water is more breathtaking than anything you can imagine.

Lagos never sleeps. Ever. It stays awake long after New York has faded in a long drawn-out yawn, matched only by the vigil of Cairo. On the Internet, the tourist board once promised:

There is something for everyone in Lagos. If your interest is sport, we have it. Soccer (football), tennis, swimming, golf, sailing—all within easy access. If you enjoy volunteer work, it's here—International Literacy Group, the Motherless Babies Home, the Pacelli School for the Blind—just to name a few opportunities. Perhaps you are a collector. You'll have plenty of chances to search for artifacts of West Africa. Masks, trader beads, artwork, woodcarving, drums, fabrics, walking sticks. You can find it all in Lagos. Own your very own beach hut on one of the local beaches. We have various clubs—both social and business—representing many nationalities. Have you ever wanted to go on a safari? Lagos is your gateway to East Africa. We offer culture in the MUSON (Musical Society of Nigeria) Centre, the German-sponsored Goethe Institute, and many other venues.

By the way a man sits smoking on the hood of his burned-out Mercedes-Benz, it is clear he wants you to know that this is all temporary. He will be rich again. By his feet a rat skulks for cover. In front of him, dead rats thrown from houses litter the street like a fresh rash of dried leaves from fall.

In front of the National Theatre, shaped like an old Yoruba crown, the statue of Queen Amina of Zaria, on horseback, sword drawn, face pulled back in a snarl, reminds you that here, women will not bow to men, I don't care what the propaganda says.

On Victoria Island, there are houses that even the richest people in the US cannot imagine owning. In Ikoyi, the money is quieter: the thing here is not the house, it is the land and the fescue lawn and the trees and the quiet swish of water against a boat docked at the end of the garden.

The poor go out of their way to drive past them. Everyone can dream.

Underneath the government-sponsored billboard that says, *Keep Lagos Clean*, a city of trash, like the work of a crazy artist, grows exponentially.

Lagos is no place to be poor, my brother.

Even though the rich don't know it or see it from their helicopters and chauffeur-driven cars, for most of the poor, canoes and the waterways are perhaps the most popular means of travel. That and the rickety molue buses.

The sign over the entrance to the open-air market announces: *Computer Mega City*. This is no joke. There is everything here from a dot matrix printer and the house-sized Wang word processors of the eighties to the smallest, newest Sony VIAO. In Lagos, it is not about what is available but only what you can afford.

The Hotel Intercontinental looks like something out of *The Jetsons*. It would be more at home in Las Vegas. Inside here, you could be in any city in the world.

In Idumota, the muezzin at the Central Mosque has to compete with the relentless car and bus horns, the call of people haggling, the scream of metal against metal, and the hum of millions of people trying to get through a city too small for them.

And yet, hanging tremulously in the heat, there it is, that

call to prayer. And all around, in the heart of the crowd, as though unseen snipers are picking them off, the faithful fall to the ground and begin praying. As though it is the most normal thing in the world—people, buses, and cars thread around them.

The Lagos Marina looks like the New York skyline. Don't take my word for it. Check Google Images.

Far away from where the heart of the city is now, you can still find the slave jetty and the slave market. Don't be fooled. A lot of Lagosians got rich selling people into slavery. It was a trade, remember?

Today, in Evanston, Illinois, I am watching a series of short films by Lagosians, and, as dusk falls over the city, listening to Fela Kuti on my iPod and drinking a soothing latte, I am listening to Lagos with my eyes closed.

The thirteen stories that comprise this volume stretch the boundaries of "noir" fiction, but each one of them fully captures the essence of noir, the unsettled darkness that continues to lurk in the city's streets, alleys, and waterways. I was honored to receive such stellar contributions from this highly talented group of writers, some very well known, some just now emerging. Together, these stories create an unchartered path through the center of Lagos and out to its peripheries, revealing so much more truth at the heart of this tremendous city than any guidebook, TV show, film, or book you are likely to find.

Chris Abani
March 2018

PART I

COPS & ROBBERS

WHAT THEY DID THAT NIGHT

BY JUDE DIBIA

Lagos Island

G*et into the house. She will be alone. Finish her!* It was not an assignment that would require taking his motley crew of two along with him. They were a nuisance most of the time—drank too much, smoked too much as well; talked excessively, always wanting to brag and to impress their silly girls who, more often than not, infected their fledgling masculinity with crabs or worse. But the two riffraff had their use. They could be relied on for aggression and fear. One of them would have to drive the bus to the house and then act as a lookout, while the other would follow him into the house. Just in case. Scorpion had since learned not to take chances.

"Cobra," he said to the gangly youth to his left, "gi' me smokes."

Cobra dug into his back pocket and withdrew a scrunched-up joint, which he put in his mouth and lit before handing it to Scorpion.

Scorpion took a long puff and then held his breath. He felt an itch on his right shoulder, the one with the tattoo of his namesake. He cursed inwardly, knowing that any time his tattoo itched it meant something was not quite right. It was like the time he had boarded the ferry from Sambo heading to the island suburb. Traffic on the road had been tight that particular day because of the rain. Jacob, the man who operated the ferry, had refused to collect money from him; but as soon as he sat down, his right shoulder began to itch persistently. He should have known that the river was hungry that afternoon and his itch was trying to warn him. The ferry capsized before they got to the shore. Jacob died, along with thirty-three other passengers.

He fingered the itch and turned around, his eyes taking in the rusty Ferris wheel and the huts that stood in front of it, built close together like the Lego bricks of a careless five-year old, the lights of the city flickering and dying in a late-evening dance of radiance and shadow. His gaze panned through all these and finally rested on the shoreline. He knew the weed was working, the way he heard the ocean roar as it swelled, threatening to swallow up all of the shore. Ah, this was good stuff! *Be still, be still, be still*, the sand seemed to whisper each time the water receded. But it was high tide. The ocean refused to be still; it took more, claimed more, and retreated less. But paradoxically, the hungry sea left behind many of its unwanted children, its vomit littering Scorpion's little patch of beachfront: a seagull's skull, uncapped beer bottles, horse scat, empty packets of cigarettes, a large shoe, a dead army of used condoms, and an old deflated football.

This was good weed! Yes, cheap gin and good weed. Was there a better way to prepare for tonight's contract? He exhaled and watched the brown smoke drift in front of him. It was blown away a moment later by a new onslaught from the high tide.

They stood by the entrance of the ogogoro shack that they had exited moments earlier. He could hear the banter of the remaining patrons, old voices ruined by years of guzzling vile liquor. He moved away and looked up into the sky, at the full moon that resembled a suspended piece of snow-white Trebor Peppermint.

"Cobra, na you go drive," he said. "And when we reach de place you go siddon inside dey watch. Sey you un'stand?"

"Yes sah."

"Razor," Scorpion said to the other one, "na me with you go enter the house-o."

Razor nodded. Much of his lean, hairless face was covered with tribal marks.

The three men headed north to where they had parked the recently serviced Kombi bus earlier in the evening. Cobra got into the driver's seat while Razor slid into the passenger seat beside him. Scorpion climbed into the back of the bus.

They did not have long to travel. The journey from the beach to the private housing estate took thirty minutes when the road was busy—they had just one bridge to cross—but at this time of night they would make it in less than half the time.

As they approached Colony Estate, Scorpion felt his tattoo itch again. The bus slowed down, which made him glance out of the window. A few feet away from the gate, a barrel-and-plank police checkpoint had been erected. Five armed officers stood in the middle of the road and motioned for the vehicle to stop. Scorpion sighed, thinking how one would expect that with the recent handover of the reins of government from the military to civilians, these boys in uniform would have finally retired to their barracks. What year did they think this was, 1993? It was the new millennium, the year 2000, and Abacha, the erstwhile military head of state, was dead! These uniformed boys were not supposed to be there, not tonight. He had been guaranteed!

The bus finally came to a halt, almost reluctantly, in a shudder punctuated by a piercing screech.

"Where you dey go?" the police officer asked.

Both Cobra and Razor remained quiet.

"I say, where you dey go?"

At the back of the bus, another officer of slightly higher rank had switched on his flashlight and was shining it through the rear window. He spotted Scorpion. Recognition flashed through his eyes before he switched off the beam and stepped away from the bus.

"Gabriel," the senior officer said, "let them through."

"But Sergeant Sule . . ." Gabriel began to protest.

"That is a command," the sergeant said. He gave a sign to the other officers to let the bus through.

Gabriel stepped back, and with a tired cough and rattle, the bus continued its journey through the gateway of the huge estate, until it stopped on the pavement opposite a two-story mansion: House 8A, Lugard Drive.

Beware of Dogs, a sign posted on the front of the guardhouse announced. It contained a picture of a vicious-looking Doberman pinscher on it.

The three men remained inside the bus. It was too bright outside. The streetlights shone like floodlights at a midnight football game, illuminating each mansion on the street, casting huge, monstrous shadows on paved streets and grass lawns.

It was so organized here. The lawns were well tended, the streets looked like one could eat off them, and the houses were neatly painted. There was not one stray dog in sight.

It still surprised Scorpion that only fifteen minutes separated chaos from harmony. This was the country they lived in, a country where a glass wall divided the rich from the poor. The rich could show off their wealth, look disdainfully at the less fortunate, and feel protected by the fragile barrier that separated them, while the poor—people from his neck of the woods—could only look on in admiration, envy, and awe.

He peered down at his watch. It was 11:58 p.m. They had only a little while longer to wait. Everything should work smoothly.

At midnight, all the lights in the housing estate went off. The streetlights flickered briefly, and then expired like tired eyes succumbing to sleep. On a normal day when electric power went off, the standby automatic generator that serviced the entire estate would come on before the residents even noticed the outage. The high price they paid to live there was no secret and their comfort was a priority. That night, however, the generator did not go on within seconds. It would not go on for another thirty minutes.

"Razor, oya!"

The two men jumped out of the bus, leaving Cobra behind. They got to the gate of the mansion and pushed it gently. It slid open with ease. There was no one at the guardhouse to stop them; there were no fierce security dogs waiting to maul them. Everything was as Scorpion had been told it would be. *Get into the house. She will be alone. Finish her!*

They entered through the unlocked door. In front of them, in the hall, was a staircase leading upstairs. They let their eyes adjust to the darkness and then to the opulence of the passageway. Thank God for the full moon that ushered in natural light, Scorpion thought, realizing also that his tattoo no longer itched. His eyes did a quick scan of their surroundings. Hanging on the walls were several portraits and photos of the couple who inhabited this haven—the radiant smiles of the handsome, bespectacled dark-skinned man and his attractive white wife bore down on him. It occurred to him just then that this hall was far bigger than the cramped rooms that whole families inhabited in his neighborhood. This had always upset him somewhat, this unrestrained waste. It was not right!

"Vincent?" a nasal female voice called out from the top floor. It was foreign. "Vincent, is that you?"

There was movement on the top floor. From where the two intruders stood, they could see a beam of light bounce off the upstairs walls and settle unsteadily on the stairs. Scorpion pulled out a long, curved knife from the waistband of his jeans. He looked at Razor and watched him uncover his own weapon—a crude nine-inch blade.

Two menacing silhouettes began a determined ascent of the stairs.

"Vin . . . Oh my God!" she screamed.

Scorpion felt the meat between his thighs stir, as if it was a man in coma shocked back to consciousness, some larva from the underworld crossing back into life.

"Oh my God! Oh my God . . . help!"

Her scream excited Scorpion all the more; made warm blood gush down to his penis. As the horror-stricken woman backed away into a room, he dropped his knife and began to unbutton his jeans. *This will not take long,* he thought. *There is enough time for this. Maybe enough time for Razor too.*

The news report was tucked away in a small corner on page twenty of the *Lagos Gazette*. Corporal Gabriel was surprised that the killing of the wife of a big man was given such a small mention in the papers. He was more surprised, though, that no one yet, not even the nosy journalists, had made the connection that in the last three months there had been six other violent robberies in the wealthy island suburb. All of them had happened in areas that usually had good security and around-the-clock power supply, yet on the nights of each raid, they had suffered electricity failures and the expensive private security officers had been nowhere in sight. The only difference with the last raid was that someone got killed. Not just anyone, but a white woman. And yet, the sensation of this had been buried on page twenty.

It bothered Gabriel that this death could have been prevented. He knew that his command post had been on duty just outside of the estate that night and had come in contact with the gang committing these crimes. He was certain that his sergeant had waved their bus into the estate. Shortly after the bus was allowed unhindered passage, the same sergeant had made them leave their post and drive to another location. When the news broke about what had happened in House 8A, Lugard Drive, Gabriel knew it was not just a coincidence.

"All these killings, it is very unfortunate," his sergeant had said to him when Gabriel went to him to discuss his suspicions.

"I believe we have a lead, sir," Gabriel pressed.

"There's no lead," the sergeant replied, looking Gabriel dead in the eye.

"That bus—"

"I said, there is no lead," the sergeant repeated. "It was just a bus."

"Yes sir," Gabriel said. He had recognized the threatening note in the man's tone. "I will leave you now."

As he made to leave, the sergeant's voice rang out, stopping him. "All of you have been doing a good job," the man said, his voice more cheerful. "I have sent something to each of your homes. I'm sure by the time you get home, your wife will have received your share."

"My share of what, sir?"

"You will see when you get home."

"I don't understand, sir. What is it for?"

"Call it motivation," the sergeant responded, smirking. "I have to keep my boys happy so you can all work better."

briel nodded slowly and left. It was not until he was outside that he realized that he had not thanked the sergeant. He wondered if the fat fool noticed or if he was too steeped in his smugness to be aware. Gabriel's suspicions only grew. He was sure it was not just some random coincidence.

When he got home later that evening, Idara, his wife, had made his favorite dish for dinner and she had made it with big pieces of chicken. Gabriel could not recall the last time he had seen chicken cut so large, not even at parties.

"What is all this?" he asked.

"Can't a woman cook for her husband?" Idara replied. "Come, sit, eat."

"You know what I mean. Can we afford this?"

"You don't have to worry. Your boss is a good man, he sent this for you." She showed him an envelope with money in it. "He sent N20,000 to us. I could not believe it!"

"What have you done?"

"Nothing. I used five thousand to shop for food and some things we need in the house."

"Why? That money is not clean," Gabriel snapped.

Idara stared into the envelope and shrugged. "Some of the notes are not so dirty."

"Damnit! Don't act like you don't know what I am saying. That money is hush money. Somebody died, Idara—"

"And so?" she cut in. "Darling, open your eyes! People die all the time. You are lucky enough to be assigned checkpoint duty on the island, and yet unlike your other colleagues you refuse to take advantage of your position. I am the only officer's wife who is poor."

Gabriel had always known his wife was unhappy about their lack of money and the finer things in life. For a long time after they got married he had been unemployed and she had been the one who'd suggested that he join the police force. She had alerted him when the police academy began accepting new intakes and had pushed him to go. For a while she had been happy, but it did not last for too long. His salary never came on time and the minimum wage they had to survive on barely got them through the month. When he was assigned checkpoint duty, she had been ecstatic. But Gabriel was not like the other officers—he preferred to do things by the book and would not take a bribe.

"Things will improve," he said.

"When?"

"I am on to something, Idara. I have been following the strange robberies taking place in some housing estates on the island."

"That is not a formal case," she said. "You shouldn't worry yourself about it."

"I think I know who the perpetrators are and I may be able to solve it."

"To what end, Gabriel?"

"Hear me out. I believe the same people committing these robberies also killed a woman. A white woman, Idara. If I lead the police to their arrest, I can get a big promotion and better financial security for us."

"What are you planning?"

He told her what he knew, about the rickety bus and the dodgy-looking occupants. He told her how he had, on his own time, visited the other places that had been hit by the robbers and how he had interviewed some of the victims who'd had face-to-face encounters with them. Those who had been willing to talk had given similar descriptions of the men. He told her that one of the victims had mentioned a scorpion tattoo. He told her he had been given the license plate number and through speaking with some local mechanics had been lucky to come across one who knew that particular bus. What he did not tell Idara was that the mechanic had been very afraid to talk about the men who had recently brought the vehicle in for repairs.

"But these people you are chasing, they sound dangerous," Idara said.

"I won't be alone when I go after them," Gabriel assured her. "I will take my findings to my superiors and request backup."

"Your superiors—you mean the nice Sergeant Sule?"

"No, I am taking this to the inspector."

Idara nodded. "Why don't you sit down and eat, your food will get cold."

Gabriel did as he was told, happy that he had almost cracked the case, optimistic that with this he could finally get the promotion he merited. As he ate, he stole glances at his wife and thought how proud she would soon be of him. Soon, she would have the husband she deserved and the respectability and perks that come with being married to a senior officer.

Scorpion was a man of very few words. He was a doer and he did. He also considered himself a righteous man. Yes, he killed people, but there was no one he had killed who did not deserve it. He could not be held accountable for killing people who plotted to kill him, or for ending the lives of rich scumbags whose very sense of entitlement ensured that the wealth of the community only circulated among themselves. He fancied himself a modern-day Robin Hood; he took from the rich. That was as much as he knew about Robin Hood, the part about stealing from the rich.

In the far corner of the dimly lit room, his men sat together smoking, drinking, and playing cards. On the floor next to them was a big canvas bag stuffed with guns and machetes. They did not have a mission that night, but Scorpion liked to always be prepared. He was not too concerned about the authorities or the police. He would ensure they were taken care of, and the ones who did not conform were taken care of in a different way. His real worry, if he were to call it that, had more to do with rival gangs, some of whom had tried in the past to encroach on his turf. The entire length and breadth of Lagos Island belonged to him; no one else was allowed to operate there.

He got up from where he was sitting and left the room. Outside it was warm and breezeless. He scratched his right shoulder with his pocketknife, almost drawing blood. It had now become an irritation for him, the constant itching. This one was more persistent than any other itch he had gotten in the past. Something big was going to happen.

Razor soon joined him outside. "Tell the others to get ready for Sunday," Scorpion said to him. "We got another hit."

When Razor nodded and returned inside, Scorpion wondered if perhaps his itch was more a warning that someone within his crew was plotting something.

Three weeks elapsed before Corporal Gabriel had enough evidence to approach the inspector. It had not been easy finding any sort of time to pursue his hunches. He worked four nights a week on checkpoint duty and had two free days in between. Well, he liked to believe that he had two off days, though the reality of being an ambitious junior officer seeking a promotion meant reporting to the station every day and being at the beck-and-call of as many senior officers as possible. He was determined to cover all grounds and check some of the information he had been given before presenting his findings to the inspector, and he knew he had to be especially careful with who he trusted at the station. It was common knowledge, after all, that some officers were in bed with criminals. In the island district he covered, there were some corporals who drove nice secondhand cars worth much more than their entire earnings in a year. Idara made it her duty to always remind him about these officers and their wives. The thought of enduring a lifetime of her nagging was enough to make him ignore his off days and check his leads.

After three weeks, he had a name for the gang leader and his possible hideout. He felt like a real detective, the kind he only encountered in movies, and this made him feel good. He had even dreamed of being promoted to the crime-solving division of the force, working in plainclothes and not the ugly black uniform of the regular police. But he saw his dream disintegrate the moment Sergeant Sule asked him about the bus that had been let into Colony Estate.

"Why, sir?" Gabriel asked.

"I hear you have some leads," the sergeant said.

This surprised Gabriel, as he had told no one in the station about what he had discovered.

"I don't understand, sir."

"You don't have to be afraid of telling me what you know. The SP himself wants us to investigate the case again and focus our energy on the people we saw in that bus."

"The superintendent?" Gabriel was unable to hide the surprise in his voice.

"Yes, the superintendent of police. He wants you on the case."

"He knows who I am?"

"Somehow he does. Look, we can stand here all day chit-chatting about who knows who, or we can get to work on the case. Now, have you heard of the gangster called Scorpion?"

"Yes, yes, I have," Gabriel replied, amazed to hear the sergeant mention the name of the man he believed was responsible for the robberies and also the murder of a harmless woman.

"What do you know?"

Gabriel told him everything, everything he had told only to his wife, everything he had intended to tell the inspector, along with everything new he had learned. As he narrated how he had pieced together the evidence, he saw what he thought was a look of admiration in the sergeant's eyes.

"I think we should storm his hideout today while we have the element of surprise," Gabriel concluded.

"No, that may not be the best idea," the sergeant said. "There is a danger that some of our men could be killed. It's his territory, after all."

"What do you suggest?"

"We have a tip-off that Scorpion and his gang plan to strike again this Sunday. We even know what estate they are targeting and which house. My suggestion is that we get there before they do and ambush them."

Gabriel agreed that the plan was a good one. It made sense to avoid the lion's den and instead pounce on Scorpion and his gang when they least expected it.

Later that evening, Gabriel was summoned once again by the sergeant for a formal briefing with the remaining five members of their squad. Sule laid out the strategy of their raid and warned all of them not to disclose it to anyone. He also took a moment to point out to the squad that Gabriel had been very instrumental in the gathering of intelligence. All this pleased Gabriel. He was certain that once Scorpion and his gang had been captured, he would indeed get the promotion he deserved.

* * *

Sunday. It came more quickly than Gabriel had imagined. The hours since he'd spoken to his sergeant seemed to have developed wings. The usually dreadful night patrol didn't bother him in the few days leading up to Sunday. He tried to contain his excitement that for once he was actually involved in real police work. Remembering the warning from the sergeant that they keep the raid under wraps, he could not tell Idara when she asked him if he had taken his discoveries to the inspector. He coded his answer to her, telling her instead that all was under control.

Before he left home on Sunday morning she stopped him by the doorway and held his hands tight.

"What is it, Idara?" he asked, sensing an aloofness in her countenance.

"Nothing," she said. "Just know that I love you."

"I love you too," he replied before leaving.

He found her action strange, but there was nothing he could do about it. He knew that in a few hours he would be able to share everything with her, perhaps including the news that he was on his way to being promoted.

At six in the evening his squad gathered, the six of them and the sergeant. Something felt odd but he couldn't put his finger on it. When he asked why they weren't given bulletproof vests, the sergeant simply said it was not required, that he had it on good account that Scorpion and his gang operated solely with machetes. Sule's tone did not invite further questioning.

They left the station before the hour struck seven. They took two vehicles, a Hilux truck and an old Peugeot sedan. Traffic on the bridge to the island was light; they got to their destination in no time. The estate's security team had been expecting them and let them in. The housing estate was like the others—gated, clean, and pretentious. They parked their vehicles away from prying eyes, in the part of the estate with the industrial-sized water-treatment facility and giant electricity generators. Gabriel imagined that, like the other housing estates that had been hit by Scorpion's crew, the occupants of this one also had no idea about the real Lagos life, about constant power failure and taps with no running water. Everything worked here. Everything here was a big lie.

"We walk to the house from here," the sergeant said.

They set off by foot. They used side streets and hidden paths, trying their best to avoid being noticed by the occupants of the estate. The houses were separated by little gardens and picket fences. Gabriel noticed basketball hoops in some yards and a child's bicycle with pink ribbons on the handlebars in another.

They arrived at a house that was far removed from the other ones. It was large, with a fancy facade, the type of house that would inevitably pique the interest of a criminal like Scorpion and his gang, Gabriel imagined. The occupants of the house were not there but the police were let in by a security guard. The sergeant instructed him to leave afterward.

Everything from then on seemed to happen fast, just like life in Lagos—the real Lagos, not the make-believe utopia of these island estates, where rich people's children rode fancy bicycles, played basketball, and had nannies and gatemen. Complete darkness came swiftly. Lagos nights could be unforgiving. They all took their places to wait. Gabriel's spot was inside the house. The others remained outside, hidden.

Just before midnight Gabriel heard a bus pull up in front of the house. His heart was racing. He checked to make sure his gun was loaded and ready. He waited to hear his squad attack the gang, to hear their barked commands for surrender and warning shots fired, but there was nothing. He wondered what was wrong. It occurred to him that maybe he had been abandoned, so he crept to one of the curtained windows in an upstairs room. And then he heard her voice: "Gabriel . . ."

It was too unreal, like something out of a bad dream. At first he thought he had imagined it, though when he shifted the curtain slightly, enough to remain hidden but still allowing him a good view outside, there she was—his wife. She was flanked by thuggish men.

"Gabriel, please come out," she called, her voice as calm as if she were at home. "No one is going to hurt you."

"Listen to your wife, Gabriel." That was his sergeant.

He peeked out of the window again and saw they were all there—his wife, his squad, Scorpion, and his gang. It suddenly dawned on him what this was: it wasn't a sting operation, it was an initiation. Everyone was in on it except him. His wife must have been the one who told the sergeant about what he'd discovered and what he planned to do with it. The night at Colony Estate must have been possible because his sergeant and squad had been paid off to look the other way. Gabriel had always known that some police officers were corrupt, but he never imagined this grand scale of deceit.

He knew he was cornered. If he attempted to be a one-man Rambo, they would surely kill him. This was not the night he would die, Gabriel thought. He had to find a way to play along and survive. His wife was out there with them. He would join her, surrender his weapon, and act like he understood the score and was in with them. After all, this was Lagos, where the police force was everybody's friend.

"Hey," Gabriel shouted out through the window, "I'm coming out!"

HEAVEN'S GATE

BY CHIKA UNIGWE

Ojo

I

Ifeatu said Reverend was the go-to guy in Lagos for anything from prayers to money. Reverend was a miracle worker, Ifeatu had said. Exactly what Emeka needed.

Reverend was not a man to be seen on a whim, Emeka's friend Ifeatu had warned him. Appointments had to be made via middlemen, who demanded a cut for their services. And then Emeka had to wait—three weeks in his case—before word was brought to him that Reverend was ready to receive him. He was given a number with which he was to identify himself at Reverend's gate before he would be let in.

"Three weeks is nothing," Ifeatu had told him when Emeka asked if Reverend was God Himself that he could keep people waiting that long. "I waited four months!" Ifeatu explained, smiling as if it were a mark of honor. "Four months, but it was worth every single second to get to see the man. Without him, I'd be nowhere."

Now, a mere two and a half years after the fortuitous meeting with Reverend, Ifeatu was living in a furnished two-bedroom flat in Surulere, running his own business manufacturing and selling sachets of pure water. In another year, he hoped to have saved enough money to build a house in his village, Osumenyi. A house with four bedrooms and a two-car garage, he told Emeka. And then he would find a good girl and marry.

"None of these Lagos girls, *ooo*. Their eyes are too open!" His own eyes twinkled with mischief. And then someday he would be a landlord in Lagos. "Imagine that—owning my own house in this city! Once Reverend sets you up, you too will be able to say the same."

Emeka thought that if Reverend could perform this miracle on Ifeatu, transforming him from the pimply faced young man who had arrived in Lagos with nothing but a plastic bag of clothes and dreams, to this fresh-faced bobo who could afford to accommodate the dreams of another man, surely he would be able to do the same for Emeka. Ifeatu, who had spent his first weeks in Lagos sleeping under the Third Mainland Bridge and begging for alms in traffic, was now the proud renter of a flat and the owner of his own enterprise, a man who could be magnanimous with his good fortune.

"You can stay as long as you want, Emeka. But I tell you, once you take off with Reverend, you won't be needing my room anymore. You'll be able to rent your own place."

The thought of having enough money to rent his own flat and buy a TV and a small generator to counteract the frequent power outages, maybe even keep a girlfriend (a Lagos girl, with hair extensions down to her buttocks; those girls who were as bold as men—Ifeatu said—in bed), filled Emeka's stomach so much that on the day he set off to see Reverend, he could not eat a single bite of food.

II

Reverend's house—it's name, Midas House, carved into a piece of sandstone above the front door—was the biggest Emeka had ever seen. It had not occurred to him before now that anyone could afford to live in a place that massive. It reminded Emeka of the cathedral in Enugu where he and his family sometimes went to church. Not in size—Reverend's house was even bigger—but in the number of religious portraits lining the walls. Emeka was ushered in by a guy wearing dark sunglasses and a beret. There were huge oil portraits of a man with a prominent scar on one cheek, flanked by Jesus, His disciples, and angels with ruddy cheeks and tie-dyed wings. In one portrait, the same man was the twelfth disciple of Jesus, his gold locket on a chain around his neck throwing off slanted rays of light, the scar on his cheek dotted with stars.

Emeka wondered if the stars had any particular significance. He was still contemplating this when Reverend walked in—Emeka immediately recognized the scar. He had expected to see a man who was as large, as expansive at least, as his reputation. But Reverend was small, no bigger than Emeka's teenage brother in Enugu. Yet unlike Emeka's brother, Reverend was dressed expensively, as if he had just emerged from a vat of liquid gold. The *LV* on his belt buckle shone bright and confident. The watch on his wrist almost blinded Emeka. The metallic thread running through his brown shirt shimmered. This was a man, Emeka thought, to whom money was of no concern. This was a man who, despite his diminutive stature, he could entrust his future to. When Reverend spoke, his voice was surprisingly, reassuringly strong.

"Everybody keeps saying I should move. Buy a house in Victoria Island or Banana Island—somewhere more upscale. I ask them, why should I move? Why move when my constituency is here. Tell me, do you think I should move?"

Emeka wondered if this was a trick question, and if it was, what was the best way to answer. Reverend did not wait for a response but continued impatiently, as if suddenly realizing why Emeka had come to see him. "So, you want to start a business?"

"Yes sir."

"What kind?"

"Taxi, sir. Or okada. I rode okada in Enugu for a while."

"And what happened?"

"The state governor banned commercial motorcycles from operating. So I came to Lagos for a second chance."

"No taxi—you have to earn a car. We'll start you with an okada since you have some experience with it. Every Monday morning at 10 a.m. sharp, rain or shine, you drop off N7,000 for me. Whatever you make on top of that is yours to keep. You do that until I tell you the motorbike has been paid off, and then you can either work for yourself or graduate to a taxi. The choice is yours. I am a fair man. I take only what's mine, but I won't be cheated. Any day you fail to make your payment, well . . ." He let the threat hang in the air unsaid.

It had been that easy. Emeka could not believe it. He wanted to shake the hand of the man who had just given him a new lease; to kneel at his feet and worship. "Thank you, sir!"

"Thank God—He's been good to me. I am reserving a space in heaven by doing good to others and following in His ways. He is a merciful God but He warns against disobedience in Leviticus 26:18—*And if ye will not yet for all this hearken unto me, then I will punish you seven times more for your sins.*"

Emeka was asked to return the next day to take possession of a brand-new motorcycle and a helmet. After, he called Enugu to tell his family the good news. His brother would be able to stay in school. His widowed mother would soon be able to retire from her petty trading. Things were on the up. "I did not come to Lagos to admire flyovers," he told his mother. "I mean business!"

III

Emeka could not remember his father. The sepia-toned pictures of him that hung on the walls of their living room did not help him to recall the man, who had died in a car accident when Emeka was seven and his mother was still pregnant with his little brother, Hope—named for their mother's optimism that her bad luck was only temporary. Emeka's father was just starting out as an independent building contractor when his bus careened off the Niger Bridge and plunged into the river. After his death, his brothers had claimed everything he owned, down to the cement mixer Emeka used to like to climb into. Emeka's mother, a woman not known for mincing words, had earned their ire by not accepting her lot quietly, and thus her family was left to fend for themselves. Emeka's mother gave birth two months after she became a widow and had no time to grieve. With Hope tied to her back, she threw herself into raising her boys and salvaging whatever was left of her husband's savings after giving him a befitting funeral. Emeka helped on weekends or whenever he had no school.

By the time he was seventeen and his little brother was ten, Emeka had quit school to help his mother full time. He had also taken over the education of Hope, teaching him to read and write while their mother cooked or attended to customers. The petty trading never yielded enough to keep the boys fed, clothed, and in school. At nineteen, Emeka apprenticed himself to an okada driver who lived in the neighborhood, and within two months he was working for the man, driving one of his motorcycles. He earned enough to supplement what his mother made, but when crime in the city rose and the government—convinced that there was a connection to the influx of commercial cyclists—banned all okadas from Enugu, Emeka found himself out of a job. He could not stay in Enugu doing nothing, watching his mother count pennies every night, so he decided to go to Lagos. Everyone knew that the only city where dreams could be pursued was Lagos. Ifeatu, who had been his classmate before Emeka quit school, had not been in the city long and already was doing very well, according to rumors. Emeka got Ifeatu's phone number from his sister, called him, and set off for Lagos with his mother's blessing the very next day.

IV

Emeka's first day as an okada driver in Lagos was so nerve-racking, so stomach-churning that he wondered if he should go back to Reverend and return the bike. He wasn't sure that he could handle putting his life in danger—Lagos drivers drove like madmen—every day. Riding in Enugu, even as a new driver, had never induced as much fear as driving in the city did. He worried that if he did not hurt himself, he would kill someone else, and so he crawled through the traffic while everyone else moved like lightning.

His first passenger complained that he would make her late for her job interview. "Why are you riding this bike like you're in a beer parlor instead of on the road? Abi, you be new driver?"

Emeka felt too shaken and humiliated to respond. But if he returned the bike, what else could he do? He could not go into the pure-water business because that was already saturated. Ifeatu had remarked that had he not started when he did and carved out a brand, it would have been impossible to make any money from it now. "Every Dick and Harry is making their own water. Some people don't even boil and filter theirs; they don't bother registering with NAFDAC. They just pour water into sachets, tie them up, and sell it as 'pure water.'"

Emeka, with no training for anything else, persevered. He clenched his teeth and went out the next day.

Okada drivers wound in and out of traffic with little regard, it seemed, for their lives or the lives of their passengers. The honking horns, the sudden brakes, the danfo drivers lurching in front of the bikes—these were all the things Emeka had to force himself to get used to if he was to make it in Lagos. He had to learn to ignore the rules, to avoid roadside markets which spilled onto the road, and to deposit his customers safely at their destinations. Amos, an older, balding man who said Emeka reminded him of his little brother, took the young man under his wing. He taught Emeka to tilt his mirrors and handlebars so he could slip his bike more easily through traffic. He taught him to be just as aggressive, just as daring as his colleagues. "If you don't, you will spend the entire day on the road without a single passenger!" He told him just how much of a bribe to give to the policemen who stopped him so that he wouldn't be too delayed. "That's their meanest punishment," Amos said of the cops. "Keeping you from working for hours if they think you are being miserly with your money. But if you give too much, you dig a hole for yourself. They'll mark you, and no policeman between here and the Niger River will ever let you off for less. Balance is the key; be wise, be a tortoise." Emeka listened, watched, and learned.

By the end of that first week, when Emeka turned in N7,000 to Reverend and still had N3,500 left over for himself, he felt like breaking into a dance. Against Ifeatu's protestations, he gave him N1,000 toward his lodging. It was not much, but it made Emeka feel less like a parasite to be able to contribute something.

By the fifth week, Emeka had shed his inhibitions. He drove as maniacally as his colleagues did, and hurled insults at other drivers in proper Lagos fashion:

Oloshi! Did you steal your license?

Madman! Who let you out of the psychiatric hospital?

Useless woman! Your father's sperm was wasted on you. Go and park that car if you can't drive it!

He sent N3,000 to his mother at the end of the five weeks and promised to send more as often as he could. He also began to keep an eye out for his own Lagos girlfriend, one like Ifeatu had. A beautiful girl he could not take home to his mother, but one who would open all the joys between the thighs of Lagos to him.

V

Emeka met Sikirat on a Friday afternoon. She had chosen him—out of all the other okada drivers clamoring for her attention—because she liked the way he looked. She told him this that very day, when Emeka dropped her off at her destination, a restaurant where she helped her aunt sell "the best jollof rice Lagos has ever seen." She would like to see him again, could he come visit her the next day at around seven p.m? The forthrightness with which she admitted being attracted to him, the fact that she would even admit it, made Emeka fall immediately in love with her. Not a single woman he knew in Enugu would tell a man she was attracted to him—it was not done. Enugu girls were raised to be demure and shy, and to never make the first move. He was not surprised that when he tried to kiss her, she kissed him back with just as much fervor. There was none of the pulling back he'd experienced with girls he had dated in Enugu. Nwamaka, his last girlfriend before he left, made him wait for two weeks before she let him give her a French kiss, annoying him by giggling when his tongue snaked into her mouth, as if he were tickling her. But Sikirat took the lead. She had short-cropped hair, a low waist, a rounded neck—not necessarily things Emeka had thought he found sexy, but he discovered that he would not have her any other way. That such women existed! That one of them had chosen *him!*

VI

Emeka was now eager for his own space. If he lived alone, Sikirat said, she might be persuaded to move in with him. Saving for a new home and buying the necessities for Sikirat (phone cards so she could call him whenever, a tight pair of jeans to bring out her curves), plus sending money home to his mother and taking care of Hope's school fees, left Emeka with hardly anything after paying off Reverend.

It was Amos who told Emeka that the only way to double—even triple—his earnings was to do the shifts that many okada men, especially the family men, did not want to do. If Emeka worked from midnight to around seven a.m., he could charge passengers up to three times the going rate. At that hour, passengers were eager to get off the streets and go home. "You are a young man. You can do this shift." The only problem, Amos warned, was that the policemen at that time of night also got greedy. They knew the okada men who worked late hours earned more, and so they doubled the bribes they asked for. "But if you make N20,000 in one night, you can easily pay a N3,000 bribe! And some men have been known to make that much."

Emeka began doing the midnight shift. He found that he liked it, being out without the sun beating every inch of him. As Amos had promised, his earnings increased so that, even with the inflated bribes he paid out to the cops who dotted Lagos at that time of the night, he still had enough to put some away. The added bonus was that during the day, while Ifeatu went out to sell sachet water, Sikirat could spend a few hours with him before going to her own job.

VII

Sikirat complained of having to make love to him in another man's house. It was as if, she said, she was in a relationship with Ifeatu as well. Besides, she was tired of squatting in another man's home. "I can't relax here," she said. Emeka promised her that he would find a flat. He was already saving for it, a one-bedroom she could decorate exactly how she wanted, somewhere she could relax. He called his mother and made promises with the reckless abandon of one for whom the world was exactly as it should be. And why not? If things continued the way they were, he would be able to pay off the motorbike and graduate to a taxi in under a year. He would be able to move Hope and his mother out of their flat—where there were pots and pans in the bedroom he had shared with Hope, and crockery under his mother's bed, because they did not have their own personal kitchen—into a better place in Enugu. He would be able to set his mother up with another business. Perhaps she could open up her own Bend Down Boutique, or BDB, selling secondhand clothes and handbags in front of the house. Sikirat's cousin had a stall in Lagos' BDB paradise, Katangowa, and could introduce Emeka to his wholesaler (who shipped in directly from Cotonou via "Ah-may-reeka").

Just three and a half months after starting the new shift, Emeka carried his first white passenger. The man's car had broken down around Obalende and he had gotten out and hopped on the first okada he saw. Emeka could not believe his good fortune. It was a slow night, as if the entire city had decided to stay indoors, and he'd begun to worry that he would return with nothing to show for it. The man directed Emeka to an address in Victoria Island. It was a long way off, not the kind of distance Emeka was comfortable traveling after midnight, especially on a night as deserted as this, but it was an opportunity he would be foolish to blow. Emeka knew that after this one passenger he could close up shop for the night. Expats were known for being generous with naira; he could easily ask this man for N10,000—and he ended up with N15,000. The extra five was: "To say thank you for saving me from a pretty rough situation." Emeka stuffed the money into his wallet, the weight of it under his buttocks giving him a buoyancy that made him fly as he rode. He could spend the next day, Sunday, with Sikirat and not worry about working. He could get the first consignment for his mother's BDB. He would take the day off, and why not? With these thoughts still running through his mind, he didn't see the police van until it was almost in front of him, cutting him off. Emeka killed his engine and waited for the cops to step out.

"Anything for the boys?"

Emeka looked around—there was only one guy. If there were others, they would have come out by now. They were like wolves, Lagos policemen. They hunted in packs. One policeman required less money. Emeka did the math and pulled out a N50 note.

The policeman laughed. "You wan play? You tink na play we dey play here?" He sounded drunk.

Emeka doubled the amount. He knew the game: you told the policeman it had been a slow day, you had a family to look after, rent to pay, and then you came to a compromise agreeable to both parties and went on your way.

"Boss, I no get more. Please."

"I fit keep you here twenty-four hours," the policeman said.

Emeka was in no hurry tonight. He had all the time to

haggle. He added another fifty. He decided that if the policeman rejected it, he would add another fifty but that was it. His mother always said that the person who holds another down to the ground must stay down too. There was no way the cop could hold him for a day. He would have to stay put as well. Emeka could play this game—he did not arrive in Lagos yesterday.

When it came, the slap blinded Emeka and threw him from his bike. "Empty dat ya wallet. You tink you can insult a whole policeman? N50, N100? You mad? Bloody civilian!" Lagos police and commercial drivers had an unwritten agreement: the latter were fair in the amount of bribes they gave, and the former never physically assaulted them. That the policeman was not playing by the rules riled Emeka. This man was not getting another kobo from him. He had been more than fair in his offer. Besides, whatever options Emeka had, emptying his wallet was not one of them. How could he give over everything he had earned that night? Fifteen thousand? He thought of the flat he had promised Sikirat they would go to next month to sign a one-year lease on. He thought of Hope's school fees he still had to pay. He thought of his mother. He thought of the N7,000 he had to give Reverend the next morning. He thought of Leviticus 26:18. He could feel his wallet deep in his back pocket, the weight of it reassuring him.

Emeka stood up. "Boss . . ."

VIII

On Monday morning, Ibukun, the president of the student union at Lagos State University, stumbled upon a corpse outside her school gate, eighteen kilometers from Victoria Island. It was that of a young man, possibly in his twenties. He had probably been killed somewhere else, most likely somewhere upscale and exclusive, and dumped where he could be just another anonymous corpse. This young man, so close in age to herself, deserved some respect, even in death. She picked up her mobile phone and dialed the police.

"This corpse you say you found, you know the person?"

"No sir."

"And so what is your business with it?"

"It's outside the school gate, sir."

"Is it inside your room?"

"No sir."

"Did you kill him? Give me your name and address."

Ibukun hung up. She knew how very easily innocent citizens could be arrested for crimes they'd had no part of. She remembered the story of her townsman who had taken the victim of a shooting to the hospital, called the police to report it, and was arrested on suspicion of being the perpetrator. Ibukun sighed and headed to class. Let the dead deal with the dead.

SHOWLOGO

BY NNEDI OKORAFOR

Ajegunle

Showlogo fell from the clear, warm Chicagoland skies at approximately 2:42 p.m.

He landed with a muted thud on the sidewalk in the village of Glenview. Right in front of the Tundes' house. There were three witnesses. The first, and closest, was a college student who was home for the summer named Dolapo Tunde. She'd been pushing an old lawnmower across the grass as she listened to M.anifest on her iPhone. The second was Mr. David Goldstein, who was across the street scrubbing the hood of his sleek black Chevy Challenger and thinking about his next business trip to Japan. The third was Buster the black cat who'd been eyeing a feisty red squirrel on the other side of the Tunde's yard.

The sight of the man falling from the sky and landing on that sidewalk would change all three of their lives forever. Nonetheless, this story isn't about Dolapo, Mr. Goldstein, or even Buster the cat. This story is about the black man wearing blue jeans, gym shoes, and a thin coat who lay in the middle of the sidewalk with blood pouring from his face.

"I go show you my logo," Showlogo growled, pointing his thick tough-skinned finger in Yemi's face. All the men sitting around the ludo board game leaned away from Yemi.

"*Kai*!" one man shrieked, holding his hands up. "*Kai*! Na here we go!"

"Why we no fe relax, make we play?" another moaned.

But Yemi squeezed his eyes with defiance. He had always been stubborn. He'd also always been a little stupid, which was why he did so poorly in school. When professors hinted to him that it was time to hand them a bribe for good grades, Yemi's nostrils flared, he bit his lower lip, frowned, and did no such thing. And so Yemi remained at the bottom of his university class. He scraped by because he still, at least, paid his tuition on time. Today, he exhibited that counterproductive stubbornness by provoking Showlogo, hearing the man speak his infamous warning of "I go show you my logo," and not backing down. Yemi should have run. Instead, he stood there and said, "You cheat! You no fe get my money-o! I no give you!"

Showlogo flicked the soft smooth scar tissue where his left ear had been twelve years ago. He stood up tall to remind Yemi of his six-four muscular frame as he looked down at Yemi's five-eleven lanky frame. Then, without a word, Showlogo turned and walked away. He was wearing spotless white pants and a shirt. How he'd kept that shirt so clean as he squatted with the other men in front of the ludo board while the wind blew the dry crimson dirt around them, no one knew. No one questioned this because he was Showlogo, and for Showlogo, the rules were always different. As he strode down the side of the dusty road, he cut quite a figure. He was very dark-skinned and this made the immaculate white of his clothing nearly glow. He looked like some sort of angel—but Showlogo was no angel.

He walked past two shabby houses and an abandoned building, arriving at his small flat in his "face me, I slap you" apartment complex. He moved wordlessly down the dark hallway, past four doors, and entered his home. It was custom for none of the flats in the building to have keys. Too expensive. Showlogo had always liked being able to just open his door. Plus, no one was dumb enough to rob him, so what need did he have for locks and keys or hiding his most valued things?

He slipped his shoes off and walked straight to his neatly made bed. Then he removed his white shirt, white pants, white boxers too. He folded and put them on his pillow in an orderly stack. He removed the diamond stud from his right ear. Then he turned and walked out. People peeked from behind doors, but not one person spoke to Showlogo or each other. Not a whisper. Unlike Yemi, his neighbors were smart.

Showlogo's meaty chest and arms were gnarled with scars, some from fighting and some from threatening to fight. Often, he'd take a small pocketknife he liked to carry, stab his bicep, and growl, "Come on!" when anyone was dumb enough to challenge him. Today, however, he didn't have his pocketknife. *No matter,* Showlogo thought as he strode down the street naked, *I go kill am.*

As he walked back to the game, people watched from food stands, cars honked at him, passersby quietly laughed and commented to each other.

"Who no go know, no go know. Showlogo know some logo-o."

"I hope say you body ready for him."

"Hope na man today. Not woman."

Everyone knew that if he said, "I go show you my logo," to a woman, it meant . . . something else. Either way, if you were smart, you knew to run. When Showlogo arrived back at the game, he found that Yemi had finally run for his life. Showlogo stood there, vibrating his chest, every pore in his body open, inhaling the hot Nigerian air.

"Why dey run?" Showlogo asked, his eyes focusing on

Ikenna, who had a big grin on his face. Showlogo sucked his teeth in disgust. "Dem no get liver for trouble."

"Please-o. Forget Yemi, Showlogo," Ikenna said, laughing nervously. "Make you calm down. He ran like rabbit. Here, take." He held a stack of naira in front of Showlogo's twitching chest.

Showlogo scowled at the money, flaring his nostrils and breathing heavily through them. Slowly, he took the stack and counted, nudging each purple-and-pink bill up with a thumb. The hot breeze ruffled the short, tightly twisted dreadlocks on his head. He grunted. It was the proper amount. If Yemi had given too little or too much, Showlogo would have left, found the disrespectful mumu, and beaten him bloody. Instead, Showlogo went home and put some new clothes on—jeans and a yellow polo shirt this time. Today, his fists would not tenderize flesh.

Showlogo owned a farm and he maintained it himself. It was good work. He'd inherited it from his adoptive father, Olusegun Bogunjoko. Twelve years ago, when his best friend Ibrahim was killed during riots between Ibrahim's clan and a neighboring clan, Ibrahim's father, who had no other male children, adopted Showlogo as his son. Showlogo had been sixteen years old. Olusegun had always loved Showlogo. The fact that Showlogo was so strong in mind and body and refused to join any side, be it a confraternity or a clan's core membership, set the old man's mind at ease as well.

Showlogo's parents had died when he was very young and he already deferred to Olusegun as a father, so the adoption made perfect sense. Showlogo took over the coco farm and ran it with the strong, attentive hand of a farmer from the old precolonial times, before oil had been discovered in Nigeria and began overshadowing all other produce, before Nigeria was even "Nigeria." Showlogo was a true son of the soil, and the death of his best friend and the love of Olusegun brought this out in him.

Showlogo worked hard on his farm, though it made little money. However, when he was relaxing and not playing ludo with his friends, he was smoking what the legendary Fela Kuti liked to call "giant mold," a very large joint that was thick at the end and thin at the tip. When Showlogo rolled one of his giant molds, his friends would call him Little Fela, and he'd smile and flex his big muscles.

Few people in Ajegunle had not heard of the great and powerful Showlogo: the Man Who Could Not Die, the Man Who Could Fight Ten Men While Drunk and Walk Away Not Bleeding, the Man Who Was Not Right in the Head, the Man Who'd Chosen to Cut Off His Ear Rather than Join a Confraternity.

He'd once jumped from a moving fruit truck just to show that he could. "I dey testing my power," he'd said as he climbed onto the truck, clamoring over its haul of oranges. "No pain, no gain. Na no know." He had asked the driver (who'd been taking a Guinness break before driving his haul to Abuja) to speed down the road. When the truck was moving forty-five miles per hour, Showlogo jumped, hit the road, and tumbled to the side of it, where he lay for several seconds not moving. His friends had run up to him, pressing their hands to their heads and wailing about how terrible Nigeria's roads were for always taking lives. But then Showlogo raised his head, sat up, stretched his arms, cracked his knuckles, and smiled. "You see now, I no fe die. Even death dey fear me."

He'd thrown himself down hills, jumped from speeding danfos, leaped from the fourth floor of an apartment building, fought five men simultaneously and won, been shot on three different occasions, lost count of the number of times he'd been stabbed or slashed with a knife, saved a friend from armed robbers by driving by and throwing a water bottle at one of their heads. Showlogo had even looked a powerful witch doctor in the face and called him *shit*. Some said that Showlogo was protected by Shango and loved by many spirits whose names could not be spoken. He only laughed when asked if this were true.

And, of course, there was not one woman who had not heard of his massive "head office." Some said that he'd once visited a prostitute and she'd given him back his money just to get him to stop having sex with her. According to this piece of local lore, the prostitute "couldn't handle his logo." Nobody messed with Showlogo and didn't regret it. Then, two days after he nearly killed Yemi, Showlogo moved from local celebrity into legend.

In Nigeria, farming no longer made one rich unless you were farming oil. So, to make ends meet, Showlogo took odd jobs. For the past two months, he'd actually managed to hold a job at the airport. He spent the day loading luggage into and off of planes. It was the kind of work he loved—physical labor. Plus, he rarely had to deal with his boss (which was when the trouble usually began for him at other jobs). The hours in the sun made his near-black skin blacker, and the loading of luggage bulked up his muscles nicely. In the two months he'd been working at the airport, he imagined he was really starting to look like Shango's son.

Keeping out of trouble at work, however, didn't mean he kept out of trouble elsewhere.

"I pay you next time," Vera said as she got off of Showlogo's okada.

Showlogo smiled and shook his head as he started the engine. "No payment necessary," he said. He watched her backside jiggling as she entered her flat. Vera wasn't plump, the way he liked his women. However, she was plump in some nicely chosen places. Showlogo chuckled to himself and drove off. It was always worth driving Vera wherever she needed to go. It was also a good way to end a long day at the airport.

He didn't make it a mile before two road police ruined his mood. He stopped at their makeshift roadblock, a long, thick, dry branch. He was shocked when the police officers demanded he pay them a bribe in order to pass.

"Do you know who I be?" Showlogo snapped, looking the two men over as if they were pieces of rotting meat.

"Abeg, give us money," one of the cops demanded, brandishing his gun, waving a hand dismissively. "Then make you dey waka!" He was smaller and fatter than the other, standing about five-six and looking like he had never seen a real fight in his life. The taller, slimmer one, who was closer to six-three, vibrated his chest muscles through his uniform and flared his nostrils at Showlogo.

Showlogo pointed a finger in the smaller man's face. "You go die today if you no turn and waka away from me now."

The moment the taller one took a step toward him, Showlogo jumped off his okada, engaged the kickstand, and stepped into the grass. He glanced at the bush behind him and then at the two policemen who were approaching. There was a red leather satchel that he carried everywhere; this way, he always had what he needed. He slung it over his shoulder and pushed it to rest on his back.

He knew exactly what he was going to do. He'd decided it as a god would decide the fate of two mere men. He slapped the smaller man across the face so hard that a tooth flew out. The trick was to open his calloused hand wide and arch his palm just so. He grabbed the other man by the balls and squeezed, then kneed the officer in the face as he doubled over.

Both men were in hot pain and bleeding, one from his mouth and one from his nose, as Showlogo wordlessly dragged them into the bush. The foliage was not dense and if there were snakes in the high grass, Showlogo didn't care. Any snake dumb enough to bite him would die, and he would not.

"Abeg," one of the policemen said as he coughed, his words wet from the blood on his lips, "let us go. Dis has gone too far. Wetin na dey do?"

"I go show you my logo," Showlogo muttered. "You asked for my logo and I go show you. Stupid set of people."

He continued dragging them for several minutes and neither man tried to fight his way to freedom. They had realized who he was; they knew better now. Soon, their bleeding slowed but they were bothered by mosquitoes buzzing around their heads. Now they stood before the trunk of a tall palm tree. Showlogo held their hands together as he brought out a coil of rope from his satchel.

The policemen never spoke to anyone about how one man was able to tie two gun-carrying officers to a tree so well that they could not undo the knots. This was understandable, because it was so humiliating. Even if it was the madman Showlogo, how could they have not tried to take him or at least run away? It was shameful. Nevertheless, this was what happened. Showlogo tied them to a tree and then returned to his okada and drove off.

The policemen were stuck to that tree for two days. No food, no water, mosquitoes and other biting insects feasting on their blood. They sat in their own urine and feces and sang songs they'd learned from the powerful and violent university confraternities they both belonged to. It was this singing that eventually attracted the group of women coming from a nearby stream. Those men could have easily died there, but luck was finally on their side.

Word about the incident spread like wildfire.

"Why you dey ask me dis nonsense again?" Showlogo said several days later. "I don move on with my life-o. Na thunder go fire those yao-yao police." He took a giant pull off his giant mold. He was sitting with his cousin Success T at the restaurant they fondly called *the cholera joint*, a plate of roasted goat meat and jollof rice in front of him. He exhaled and grabbed his spoon with his left hand and shoveled rice into his mouth. It had been a long day of work at the airport and the food tasted like heaven. "Next time they will stay out of my way," he added through his mouthful.

"People dey talk about it," Success T said, smiling. He was the only person on earth Showlogo trusted. The two had grown up together and then lived in the same flat for years when they were older. Both even had access to each other's bank accounts. "How you dey tie them? Everyone wants to know."

Showlogo paused as he ate more rice and drank from his bottle of Coca-Cola. He belched loudly and pounded a fist against his chest. "I be One Man Mopo. I no need help and no dey fight in group," he responded, biting into a piece of goat meat. "You no believe me?"

"I do," Success T said. He leaned forward, the smile wiped from his face. "Showlogo, I no want make you go to jail. Those police be cultist. Their people haven't forgotten-o."

Showlogo chewed his goat meat and smiled. "Jail no be

for animal. Na for human person. But don worry. Jail no be for me."

He wasn't stupid. He thought about it. The police always had each other's backs. And they held grudges like old women. And the fact that those two idiots who'd had the nerve to ask him for bribes were also part of confraternities was not good. So Showlogo decided to lay low for a bit. No partying or playing ludo outside with his friends for a few weeks. Go to work and then go home, that was the plan.

Then the Igbo shop down the street was robbed. Showlogo held his phone to his ear as he got on his okada that evening. Hearing about the incident first, Success T had called to warn him. "Watch out, o!" Success T said. "That kobo-kobo Igbo shop nonsense. Word on the street is that they caught the guys who did it and they said they knew you." Showlogo blinked. Time to disappear. He would stay with Success T for a day or so until he figured out a better place to go for a while. He put the phone in his pocket and quickly drove home.

As he tried to pack up a few things, he heard cars arrive outside his building. When he looked out his window, he saw that one of the men who exited the police car was the very cop he'd left to die in the bush, the one with the fat wobble-wobble belly. They'd arrest him, and once in police custody Showlogo knew they'd find all sorts of reasons not to release him. He'd rot in jail for months, maybe years. He escaped from the back of the building just before the police came to his flat's door.

He fled to the most hidden place he could think of—the airport tarmac. The shaded area beneath the mango tree on the far side of the strip was where the luggage loaders took their breaks. He'd once spent a night here when he was too tired to go home. Now, he sat down on the dirt to eat the jollof rice he'd bought from one of the lady vendors on his way there. He leaned his back against the tree and let out a tired sigh, thinking about his flat. Would the police force their way in and ransack the place?

As he sat in the early-evening darkness, chewing spicy tomato–flavored rice, Showlogo made a decision in the way he made every decision: fast. He stared at the 747 across the tarmac. He knew the schedule; this one would soon be bound for America. It was still glistening from its most recent wash. The water droplets sparkled in the orange and white airport lights. The airplane looked fresh, new, and it was headed to new lands. The sight of the clean airplane combined with the spicy rice in his mouth made the world suddenly seem ripe. Full of potential. Offering escape. For a while. He drank from his bottle of warm Coca-Cola and the sweetness was corrupted by the pepper in his mouth. He smacked his lips. He'd always liked this combination.

An hour later, he bought another container of rice from the same woman, demanding that she pack it into the plastic container he normally used to carry his toothbrush, toothpaste, and washcloth when he worked late hours. He went to his locker and brought out the heavy jacket he used when he worked during chillier nights.

"Success T, how far?" he asked, shrugging on the jacket as he held his phone to his ear.

"I'm good," Success T said. "I dey study. You dey come out with us tonight. Where are you?"

"Look, I'm going for a little while. These yao-yao police need to calm down. Have Mohammed and Tolu watch my farm."

"Where no dey go?"

"Away."

After a pause, Success T said, "Good. I dey call you before. Some police dey wait outside your place. I drove by half hour ago."

"Make you no worry about me. I fine."

After the call, Showlogo stared out at the tarmac and pushed his phone deep into his pocket. He moved quickly. It was dark but he knew where he could walk and remain in the shadows. The New York–bound 747 would be pushing off soon, so he had to be quick. He climbed up the undercarriage, pressing a foot against the thick wheel. He hoisted himself into the plane's landing-gear bay. In the metal space around him there were wires, pipes, levers, and other machinery.

He positioned himself in a spot where the wheels would not crush him and he could hang on to a solid narrow pipe. He'd have to grasp it tightly upon takeoff because the bay would fill with powerful sucking air as the plane picked up speed and left the ground. "One Man Mopo," he said aloud with a laugh as he practiced his grip. He positioned his satchel at his back. Inside it were his phone, charger, the container of rice, a torch, his wallet, and a few other small things. All he'd need.

Showlogo's mind was at ease when the plane began to move. In a few hours, he'd be in the United States. He'd never dreamed of going there. Nigeria was his home and the city of Lagos was his playground. But he understood change and that it could happen in the blink of an eye. He'd learned this when he was seven years old: one day his parents had been there, then the next, they'd died in a car crash. Since then he'd learned this lesson over and over. One day Chinelo had loved him, the next she was marrying his cousin and pretending she didn't know him. One day there was food to eat, the next there was none. One day he had no money, the next his pockets were stuffed with naira and he had two jobs. One day he could buy fuel for his car, the next his car had been stolen and this didn't matter because there was a fuel shortage. He'd lived his life this way, understanding, reacting to, and riding the powerful and weak waves of the universe's ocean. He was a strong man, so he always survived.

The plane taxied to the runway. Showlogo watched the passing black pavement below. Success T would keep his flat for him, maybe use it as a second home when he wanted to be alone. Success T lived a fast life and was always sneaking away to spend days in remote hotels to get away from it all; the idea that his cousin could now use the place was comforting.

Of course, Success T would have to get rid of the police first. Showlogo chuckled to himself when he thought of the cops who were probably still waiting for him outside his home. They would spend weeks trying to find him. He'd lose his job at the airport by tomorrow morning and be replaced by the afternoon. So be it. He would be elsewhere. Who no know, no go know.

Showlogo began to have second thoughts as the plane picked up speed. The suction in the landing-gear bay was growing stronger and stronger . . . and stronger. *Oh my God*, Showlogo thought. He looked down at the pavement below. It was flying by, but maybe he could still throw himself out and survive. The plane wasn't even off the ground, but already he felt an end to his strength. It was too late.

Whooosh!

When the plane left the ground, Showlogo felt as if he were dying. Every part of his body pressed against the bay's metal walls. The air was sucked from his lungs. As the earth dropped away from him, his world swam. But this sense of death only lasted about thirty seconds. Then his body stabilized. In the next few minutes, Showlogo marveled at the fact that he would never be the same again. Who could be after feeling what he felt, seeing what he was seeing? Nigeria was flying away from him.

As the temperature rapidly dropped, he pulled his thin coat over himself and thanked God that he'd worn his best and thickest jeans, socks, and gym shoes. The undercarriage retracted. The clouds and distant earth below were shut away as the metal doors closed and Showlogo was pressed in tightly. "Shit!" he screamed. There was so much less space than he'd expected. And the temperature was still dropping.

He shivered. "Sh-Sh-Showlogo no go sh-sh-shake. No sh-sh-shaking for Sh-Sh-Showlogo," he muttered. Only a few yards above him, people sat in their cushioned seats, warm and safe. The flight attendants were probably about to offer drinks and tell them about the meal that would be served. Showlogo had flown twice in his life. The first time was to Abuja, with his parents when he was five. When his parents were still alive and telling him every day what a great doctor he would be. The second time was a few years ago to Port Harcourt, when his parents were long dead and he had business to take care of in Calabar. On both flights, he remembered, they'd served snacks. When he was five, it had been peanuts or popcorn. As an adult, it had been drinks and crackers. Success T told him that on international flights, there was an actual meal.

"It was shit," Success T had laughed. "For this small-small plate, the beef wey dem put dey tasteless-o! If I chop am, I go die before we reach Heathrow!"

Success T wasn't exaggerating. He had been born with intestinal malrotation and lived on a very strict diet of seafood, fruits and vegetables, and very selected starches. He could not eat fufu or foods soaked in preservatives, and he could not eat most European and American cuisine. As Showlogo thought of his cousin, who was practically solid muscle and scared anyone he competed against in boxing tournaments, yet could be felled by merely eating the wrong food, he chuckled. Then he shivered again. He brought out his flashlight and flicked it on. The beam was dim despite the fact that he'd put in fresh batteries less than two hours ago.

He could see his breath as if he were smoking a giant mold. Speaking of which—he reached into his satchel and brought it out. He had to flick his lighter ten times before it produced a weak flame, then he only managed three puffs before it went out. The vibration of the plane's engine shook his freezing body, causing his legs and arms to flex. He squeezed his palms and curled his feet and toes. He flexed his buttocks and straightened the tendons in his neck. Time was slowing down and he felt calm. He could see the black borders between the frames. Slowly, he ate his jollof rice, wheezing between bites. It was warm, red, and spicy, heating his belly. Then he lay back and thought of nothing more.

As Showlogo lay on the sidewalk, the woman named Dolapo Tunde, the man named Mr. David Goldstein, and the black cat stared. Dolapo shuddered as she grasped her lawnmower. She shuddered again and crossed herself. Then she pulled out her blue earbuds and let them fall to her thighs. Mr. Goldstein dropped his soapy sponge and leaned against his Chevy Challenger. All thoughts of work fled his mind as he tried to piece things together.

The man could not have fallen from any house or building. There wasn't one close enough. No tree either. He'd fallen from the damn sky! But Mr. Goldstein had seen photos on the Internet of what was left of people who leap from tall buildings. He'd seen one of a man who'd jumped from a skyscraper. The guy had been nothing but mush in the road. So Mr. Goldstein shuddered as well, for he did not want to see or even know what the man looked like underneath.

Only Buster the cat was brave and, of course, curious enough to inspect. He padded across the road. He hesitated for only a moment and then he walked right up to Showlogo's body and sniffed the side of his head. Buster looked at the man's nose, which was pressed to the concrete and dribbling blood. The smell of the blood was rich and strong—very, very strong. Buster had never smelled blood with such a powerful scent. He was focusing so hard on the rich bloody aroma that when Showlogo grunted, the cat was so deeply startled that he leaped four feet in the air.

Across the street Mr. Goldstein shouted, "Holy shit! HOLY SHIT! Whoa! He's alive! How the *fuck* is that dude alive? What the hell!"

Showlogo lifted his head and glanced around. He coughed and wiped his bloody nose. He sat up, stretched his arms, cracked his knuckles, and smiled tiredly. He looked at Dolapo, who was staring at him with her mouth hanging open. His brain was addled, so when he spoke, what came out was not the pidgin English he meant to speak, not even the Standard English he should have spoken, for he was most certainly in America. Instead, he spoke the language of his birth, Yoruba.

"You see? I can never die," he said. "Even death fears me."

Dolapo tried to reply, but all that came out was a gagging sound.

"I agree with you," he said to her. "There are better ways

to travel. Can you prepare some yam with palm oil for me? I have a taste for that."

Dolapo stared at him for several more seconds and crossed herself again. Then she quietly responded to him in Yoruba, "God is with me! I have no reason to fear evil. Be gone, fallen angel! Be gone, devil!" She switched to English. "In the name of Jesus!"

Showlogo stared blankly at her and laughed. "My eyes tell me I'm in America, my ears tell me something else." He stretched his back and began to walk up the sidewalk. He was Showlogo, and he could survive anything and anywhere. Behind him Buster the black cat followed, attracted and intrigued by the strongest-smelling blood he'd ever sniffed.

JUST IGNORE AND TRY TO ENDURE

BY A. IGONI BARRETT

Egbeda

1

Every night since the first night he spotted it on his doorstep, the big brown rat had been climbing the stairway to the man's front door to gnaw his potted dwarf oyster plant. The man only noticed the damaged leaves nineteen days after that first visit, during which time he had tried twice to poison the rat. On both occasions the toxic morsels, which he arranged like Babylonian sacrificial offerings along the ziggurat of his stairway before locking up for the night, remained untouched the following morning, and when he flung open his door each night he saw the rat skittering away. The question arose: if the creature was shrewd enough to shun death in the crayfish-smelling guise of PowerKill™ powder and Commando™ pellets, why then would it persist in coming back?

The first time the man came upon the snooping rodent he had been frying sweet potatoes and egg sauce for a bachelor's dinner and he'd supposed its appearance at his door was a compliment to his cooking. Subsequent sightings soon soured his disposition toward the thief scheming to sneak into his house. That was the juncture at which he abandoned his psychic negotiations with the reconnoitering rogue by deciding to poison it, but after his two attempts failed to end its life, or even its nighttime visits, the man's anxiety grew large enough to accommodate the urban myth of the indestructible Lagos rats. Human logic was reinstated on a Sunday morning when the man was watering his potted garden and discovered that his foe had a fondness for snacking on the green and pink leaves of the dwarf oyster plant decorating his landing. So he followed this synaptic trail to its QED, dug up the houseplant, and threw it away. That same night around eleven o'clock the front door banged open, the rat clambered out of the desolate flowerpot, scurried across the landing with its bulky testicles swinging, and bounded down the staircase for the last time.

But on Monday morning the man awoke to the invasion of his territory and the first salvo in open warfare: a round hole in the mosquito netting of his kitchen window and Tic Tac–sized droppings scattered around his overturned garbage bin.

2

Sometime during the fifteenth year of the twenty-first century, an outbreak of Lassa fever struck terror in the imaginations of the human population of Lagos, causing them to declare war on the rats. For months every corner of the city was shaken by desperate battles that pitted neighbor against neighbor and left the streets littered with tire-squashed carcasses. But even before this conflict slipped the pin from the grenade of the Lagosians' pent-up frustrations, their treatment of rodents already resounded for its cruelty. Anyone can empathize with humanity's primal urge to hunt for thrills, to slaughter off entire populations and wear their skins as fashion fads, to collect their ears for charms and their teeth for potions and mount their heads on walls as trophies. Everyone knows we need guinea pigs for research, lab rats to inject and dissect for medical tests, military experiments, psychological studies, the endless pursuit of knowledge; and everyone knows we need to breed hairless cats to show off at cocktail parties and brachycephalic lapdogs to carry around in handbags because—same as zoos, safari parks, aquariums, and bullfight pits, a.k.a. animal prisons and killing grounds—these cheer us up.

Yet no one in Lagos knows why it became acceptable for rat-poison hawkers to hang dead rats from strings and strut through the crowded streets blowing their whistles as they swung these lurid advertisements in people's faces. Perhaps the answer to this vulgarity, the impetus for such strident displays of human nastiness, lies in the creeping suspicion that we've already seen defeat in a war whose sideline battles we are still fighting. For anyone can see that Lagos is a city of rats—they far outnumber the twenty million human inhabitants. They live in our homes, feed better than we do on our waste, and adapt more quickly to the poisons and anthropogenic microbes wiping us off the earth. Even today no map of Lagos would be complete without a rat's-eye view of the garbage landfills and trash-choked canals, the mechanic workshops bursting with metallic skeletons dusted in rust, the polluted subsoil devoid of plant root networks, the crumbling foundations of concrete constructions, the underground labyrinth of household septic tanks leaking sludge into the groundwater. The rotting underbelly of the city we built for the rats.

3

The man worked as a store manager and mattress salesman at a Vitafoam depot in Surulere, which was where he'd lived before moving to Egbeda. For 693 days he had shared a small apartment—two connected rooms, a kitchen, and an outbuilding bathroom—with three men, each of them contributing N180,000 to make up the one-time payment of two years' rent. His relationship with these other men, which was cordial during the courtship and honeymoon of their ménage à quatre, deteriorated into a mismatched tug-of-war. All three pulled on one side toward domestic insouciance and soiled dishes in the kitchen sink, while he spent too much time picking, sweeping, and washing up after them. When their avowals of gratitude changed to constant banter about his WALL-E status versus their pigpen nature, he realized the living arrangement wouldn't work for his peace of mind.

Housing in Surulere was too pricey for him to go it alone, so he ignored his discomfort and endured the others' untidiness until the rampaging mice began to bear litters in his clothes. Before that final affront he had continued ducking the flying cockroaches in the mildewed bathroom and squishing centipedes among the streamers of wet tissue paper littered around the toilet bowl; he had ignored the eternal armies of stinging ants foraging across the greasy kitchen floor, and endured zinging houseflies in daylight hours, singing mosquitoes at night; and though he couldn't ignore it, he had endured the pheromone stench of rat piss from the ceiling where they scrabbled and squeaked through the night. But after that workday morning when newborn mice—blind and pink-skinned, their open mouths suckling air—tumbled out of his folded trousers, he decided he had endured too much.

4

Many years before, when the man was still a boy, he'd visited for three weeks with his late mother's older sister in a rat-haunted house beside a canal in Surulere. That was his first trip away from home, his first sighting of apples outside the pages of school primers—he bought two from the rowdy hawkers thronging the tollgate into Lagos, and stashed one inside his rucksack before crunching into the other—and the last time he grew attached to an animal.

His aunt was a nurse at the hospital on Randle Avenue, and she got a cat around the time of her nephew's visit so he wouldn't be home alone when she worked nights. It was a brown-and-white tabby kitten whose thin haunches and ragged coat made it look underfed. In the first days after the boy's arrival—before his aunt's habitual absence induced him and the cat to become partners in surrogacy who sought each other out for play, toilet training, and feeding duty—it meowed almost nonstop at night for no apparent reason until the boy became convinced it also missed its mother. He discovered many things about his feline chum during those weeks of their deepening dependency: the switchblade claws that talked back via scratches on his skin; the interior monologue of purrs drumming its chest under his stroking hand; the coupled twitching of its radar ears and periscope tail in response to his copycat meowing; the sandpaper tongue that tickled his food-stained fingers. He also cracked the riddle of the cat's crying at night, which it did for the same reason he had a hard time sleeping: because of the hordes of rats that ghosted about the house after the lights were dimmed. They poured in from the trash-heaped banks of the canal with as much ease as the fetid vapors rising from its blackish waters. Their presence wasn't as obvious at sundown or as bold in daytime, but they still left their traces, same as the headache the boy got from the relentless stench on the first morning he awoke in that house to find a gnawed hole in his rucksack and his second apple missing. As a protection against rat attack, but also spurred by loneliness and his pity for the frightened mewling, the boy began bringing the cat into his bed at night. His aunt noticed soon enough how well he slept with the kitten curled up beside him; she got into the habit of praising herself to friends for her parenting insight every time she left him at home. She would remember this detail when the boy had become a man and paid her a visit in Surulere after he'd settled in Lagos. She also remembered how she was repaid for her selflessness: how the boy bawled like a brat when it came time to travel back to his father's house, how he kept begging despite her warnings that he control himself, how he accused her of being a bad aunty for refusing to allow him to take the cat. These forgotten memories were rekindled on the same day the man told her about his rat problem in Egbeda and that he was thinking of getting a kitten, to which the aunt replied, "No, that won't work. The rats in Lagos are too big for kittens, and they're smart too, they kill them before they grow." She knew because she had lost four kittens before she learned. The rats came at night and tore out their throats, she said. "I never told you, but that's how your friend, my first cat, the one I got when you stayed here as a child—that's how it died."

5

At eighty-one years old, the landlady looked and smelled like a beached whale. Flesh hung in folds of blubber from her belly and thighs, though not her arms, which were like bloated bags of adipose; and she was stooped over as if from the weight of all that fat. Her decaying odor pounced on the man as soon as she opened her door to him and the agent, and all through her rambling conversation about the terms of his tenancy—which somehow included her disjointed narratives about who she was (a true-born child of Isale Eko, daughter of the soil, and a blood sister to the royals of the land), and how much wiser than him she was because she had buried four stillborn children who, had they lived, would all be older than him—

he kept fighting off her smell's suffocating grip on his throat. Her wrinkly face was splotched by eczema, which she raised her hands to scratch as she talked, and the blue nightdress she wore was food-stained across the chest and browned with grime about the haunches. And yet her living environment wasn't untidy. The paved ground of her fenced and gated yard was swept clean and kept free of cracks. The building itself—a seventies oil boom–style house with identical large apartments on two floors and a smaller upstairs apartment at the rear—was in good repair for its age. The paint job looked recent, the windowpanes were all intact, the cube-shaped cavities left in the walls by the air conditioners of previous tenants had been plastered over, and the arrangement of the external plumbing pipes and electrical wires conveyed the sense that shoddy workmen hadn't gone unsupervised. The man admired the sturdiness of the building, he appreciated the clean surroundings, and after the agent collected the key to the vacant rear apartment from the landlady and led him there, he decided he wanted it. He had seen many shapes and sizes—and prices too—in all the months of house searching across the choked heart of Lagos, but this was the first place he saw that ticked all his boxes. Indoor bathroom, running water, detached compound, wide windows, and cross-ventilation, plus the bonus of a top-floor view, all his for just under N50,000 more than his budget.

One counterweight to his euphoria at finding a worthy house he could borrow money to afford was the rush-hour traffic he would encounter two times a day on the commute between Egbeda and Surulere. Another was the hike in his transport costs, not caused by recurrent fuel scarcity, but due to the farther distance between home and workplace. A third drawback, perhaps, for this Surulere wannabe was the strangeness of Egbeda's market-town character. The noise, the clash of smells, the cram of all types of peddlers and all sorts of stores: Egbeda had everything Surulere didn't want. The man wanted everything Surulere had. But since the one thing he wanted more than anything else was in Egbeda, he swatted his doubts aside, and ignored the questions plucking at his subconscious about the cheapness of the two-bedroom, about why such a first-rate property had remained empty so long that the dead gecko on the kitchen counter had almost crumbled into dust. When the agent's selling voice declared that a bunch of people were lined up to steal his luck if he didn't seal the deal that day, the man broke his silence, confirmed he would take the house, and followed the agent into the landlady's ground-floor apartment to endure her putrid stench for the second of many times to come.

6

The man's house hunting led him to Egbeda out of necessity rather than choice. First he looked in Surulere, as he worked there, but also because he had lived there long enough to grow blind to its ugly side. It helped as well that Surulere, unlike many newer districts of Lagos, was connected to the public waterworks. Power supply, too, appeared steadier in Surulere than anywhere else he had slept in the city. As for garbage collection on his street, it was provided by private contractors for anyone who paid their fees, and the stink-bomb trucks arrived every Thursday—even in the rainy season when flash floods swept away roads across the swampland of Lagos, but left his street intact because it was tarred. Public facilities still existed in Surulere, albeit in an enfeebled state, and despite its high cost of housing and its teeming rat population, the man believed the devil he knew was his best chance of finding paradise.

Thus he trudged the familiar streets after work and on Sundays, searching with a stranger's gaze for chalked signboards announcing miniflat vacancies, or one-bedroom apartments for rent, even single rooms to let, all of which he found he couldn't afford. Yet he kept on looking for any place that would accept his life savings of N200,000; he searched, and pleaded, and tried, and tried again. He sought out the landlords of those single rooms closest to his budget to beg that they accept six months' rent in lieu of the customary two years up front. Weeks of trying that path only confirmed there was no hope there, especially for a citizen who was seen an outsider by the Yoruba landowners. The man changed tactics: he knocked on the gates of houses along the genteel axis of Adelabu Road, Ogunlana Drive, and Adeniran Ogunsanya Street to ask the tenants if they would consider subleasing their unused gatehouses and boy's quarters. When this route only succeeded in proving how afraid of strangers Lagosians are, he tried again by ingratiating himself to the construction workers toiling at building sites (he bought them bags of ice-cold pure water, a bribe worth more than cash under the lash of the afternoon sun) before plying them with questions about the architect's plan—all these efforts undertaken for information, for an early look-see, for a fighting chance of slipping his foot in the doorway before the arrival of those procurers whose business cards bore the title of housing agent.

He only gave up on Surulere after he realized that rival salesmen in a seller's market are always members of a secret society of mutual benefit. It seemed every single one of the local brotherhood of housing agents knew him either by sight or reputation, and when these men began to ignore his phone calls or greet his appearance at their dingy offices with expressions of weary disdain, he expanded his search to nearby

Mushin and Oshodi. But even in these hardscrabble districts his budget remained as much an obstacle as his ambitions. A man who couldn't raise more than N210,000 and yet insisted on his right to amenities like kitchen plumbing, an indoor toilet, and, in the curious case of the hole-in-the-wall room he inspected on a dirt road that straddled the boundary between Oshodi and Agege, windows wide enough to escape through in case of fire. Agent after agent turned him away upon becoming convinced that he was pickier than was acceptable in a Nigerian. The few who pitied him enough to show him the slum shacks befitting his pocket were afterward outraged at his lack of appreciation. He would rather be homeless than waste his money on those rat and cockroach playgrounds in face-me-I-face-you houses, he said. Life in Lagos was dangerous enough without sleeping in those hovels that turned into gas chambers once the I-pass-my-neighbor generators came on, he told them. When one of these 10 percent–chasing agents began reproaching him about being too proud for a poor man, he riposted: "Yes, I agree, but how is that a bad thing?"

7

Eight hundred years later, when the history of Eko is taught to our children, they will never understand why we did what we did. Their teachers will try to explain: *Those were strange times in Lagos; everybody was a criminal.* This textbook opinion, unwarranted though it may seem now, will nevertheless be reinforced throughout their childhood with stories and images in twenty-ninth-century multimedia. This is the truth we are not yet able to see in twenty-first-century Egbeda: a typical Lagos neighborhood—the air poisoned by generator fumes, the treeless landscape strewn with plastic trash, the waterways turned into festering sewers—so crowded with government-forsaken people and makeshift infrastructure that it is already under threat of being expunged from the urban planning models. Ikoyi and Surulere, the former more affluent and the latter middle class, are two sides of the past face of Lagos. Traffic-jammed Ikeja and flood-prone Lekki are likewise two extremes of the city's present face; while the seaside facade of Eko Atlantic City is the future that Lagos is waterskiing toward. Thus Egbeda, like several other haphazard Lagos districts, is stuck in the perilous place of having no past glory, no present amenities, and no future plans. We would feel sorry for the residents who live with this foreboding, who leave their homes every sunrise with the nagging dread that this might be the day the bulldozers come and their neighborhood goes. We would feel sorry if we didn't already know that most of them, the residents of Egbeda, like everyone else in Lagos who litters plastic bags and leaves their tungsten lightbulbs burning in daylight hours, is complicit in the crime of destroying our mother planet.

8

The man almost didn't go to see the house in Egbeda. This was partly due to the agent but mainly because he had never been to that section of the city in his time in Lagos, and so all he knew about it was what he'd heard about the endless traffic jams of vehicles and people. He found out about the vacancy from the agent, who led him to the outsized birdhouse masquerading as a human habitation in the no-man's-land between Oshodi and Agege. That disappointment colored the man's perception of everything the agent promised afterward. Which was why, when the agent snapped his fingers in a feigned eureka and began spieling on about another perfect place in far-off Egbeda, the man responded by laughing in his face long enough to hurt his feelings. The agent shut up and showed the man two other places around Oshodi, neither of which even deserved excuses for turning them down. When the man remarked on the agent's lack of enthusiasm for what he was selling, the rejoinder was a furious accusation about those who have ears not hearing and eyes refusing to see. This outburst ended with the agent swearing on his grandmother's grave about the oh-so-rightness of the two-bedroom upstairs apartment that was a giveaway at N220,000 for a year's rent, excluding the agent's fee. Faced with the choice of finding another agent to start looking all over again, the man decided the better path was the high road of pacifying this charlatan into discharging his duties with some modicum of goodwill. That's why he agreed to see the house in Egbeda.

9

In today's Lagos, without money to buy your way, ideals of comfort are impossible to find. The man admitted this to himself after he had suffered enough of the landlady's smell. She kept him waiting sixteen days into the contractual start of his tenancy before handing over the key to his apartment. During that fretful period he traveled over from Surulere to pay her five separate visits, none lasting less than two hours of one-sided chatter and remorseless bruising of his olfactory senses. The first time she insulted him was on the second of these visits. He had interrupted the rerun of her life story around nine o'clock to say he needed to start heading back to Surulere because he had work tomorrow, upon which her tone sharpened into anger as she called him a disrespectful Igbo man. That night his sole response was, "I am not Igbo," but even such anodyne assertions of fact were enough to tip her into boiling rages, as he experienced on every visit afterward until he gained his key. Whenever the spirit moved her, her mouth became as offensive as her odor.

In the early weeks of his occupancy the man thought *he* was the problem, that something he did or didn't do had turned her off him, some cultural blindness on his part perhaps, like not bowing his head when he greeted her in his stilted Yoruba; or calling her *Alhaja* (the honorific the agent had addressed her by) rather than *Mama* as most people did; or not offering to carry her shopping bag the evening they met at the gate as she returned from buying smoked fish around the corner. He ceased overcompensating in his attitude toward her (mainly by surrendering his time to the black hole of her loneliness) only after the first furtive visit from his neighbor, the woman who lived in the front upstairs apartment. Before she showed up at his door he saw her every weekday morning for six weeks as she drove off with her two children—she dressed for work, they for school—in her beat-up Nissan sedan, and yet, without fail, every time he greeted her, she only nodded, never spoke. But that night in his apartment, with the louvers closed for privacy, she apologized for her seeming rudeness. It was because of the landlady, who would accuse them of gossiping about her if she saw them together. It was a pattern the neighbor said had played out countless times in the nine months she had resided in this building, and now that she was counting down to the end of her tenancy, she hoped to avoid repeats until she moved out. As penance for her cowardice she told the man everything she knew about the old woman, filling in the missing parts of the life story he had heard over and over from a source whose sincerity he had always sniffed at. The neighbor spoke about the landlady's instant mood changes, her paranoia about everything, her deceitfulness over anything, her gaping lapses in logic, her willingness to employ aggression in word and action at any chance she got—most of which the man already knew through hard-won experience, though what he didn't know was that everybody knew. When the neighbor confirmed she had gotten her apartment through the same agent who led him into this trap, the man realized he had before him all he needed to answer his own questions about how he found what he was looking for in Egbeda. There was nothing left to talk about, end of story; and so the landlady's prisoners wished each other good night.

10

That same night, as the man was taking out the garbage after frying sweet potatoes and egg sauce for a late dinner, he saw the big brown rat on his doorstep for the first time.

PART II

IN A FAMILY WAY

THE SWIMMING POOL

BY SARAH LADIPO MANYIKA

Victoria Island

Luke Adewale, president and CEO of Competent Communications, died suddenly and unexpectedly after a tragic fall at his home residence on Friday. He was sixty years old, and expired after sustaining severe injuries. In addition to his dedication to his beloved wife, daughter, and the rest of his family, he was also an avid gardener, amateur swimmer, and self-made house designer. In his limited free time, he enjoyed evening strolls, table tennis, and watching sports, in particular Chelsea F.C. He was a dedicated and humble church member and was passionate about supporting causes that improved the lives of young girls and women. An ocean of condolences immediately began to pour in as soon as his passing was announced.

Speaking of oceans, Victoria Island is slipping into the Atlantic, but nobody wants to know. People have other, more pressing things to worry about. Take Mr. Adewale, for example, who, on his last day, while having breakfast, complains most vociferously about the neighbors. Would he have done so had he known that the next day these same neighbors would be wailing at the news of his death? But in that moment, as in every moment of his life, his own death fails to cross his mind. His audience, Mrs. Adewale, gently reminds him that where they live is still considered the crème de la crème of Lagos, which brings Mr. Adewale no comfort.

He built his Victoria Island mansion in 1991, and deems every house constructed thereafter an encroachment—a mass of higgledy-piggledy dwellings conspiring to block his ocean view. So no, Victoria Island is *not* the crème de la crème. Not anymore.

"Listen," he says, opening the sliding doors so that the wife might better hear the roar of the neighbor's pneumatic drill and the drone of generators.

"Yes, dear. Please close it," she sighs, slapping about her legs in expectation of mosquitoes let in from outside.

"You see what I mean?" he presses, impatiently kissing his teeth. "All of this random construction with no zoning laws, no building codes, and no thought for aesthetics! Is this the sort of legacy we want to leave for our children?" He believes he's made his case, oblivious to the fact that his wife is bored with the topic and especially bored with him.

Mrs. Adewale finds her husband's ramblings tiresome and pedantic, and the reference to children irritating. She sometimes wishes he'd just hurry up and die. He's grown fat in recent years and prone to wheezing. One would think that in such a state . . . and yet the man lives on. Things might have been more tolerable if only she had someone to complain to, but her friends are jealous. They wonder why she isn't content with her wealthy husband. Who cares if she's never been able to bear the man a child, or that the inherited daughter from the man's first marriage is trouble? The girl is away at boarding school most of the time, so what's the problem? But never mind these friends. She'll soon put all of this behind her.

The inheritance now joins them for breakfast, to which Mrs. Adewale reacts with her habitual withering glance, envious of the ease with which the girl wears her low-rise jeans and sequined tank top. It's not a look meant for middle-aged women, but Mrs. Adewale has occasionally tried squeezing herself into such things, maddened that her youth and beauty are slipping away just when the new pastor has taken an interest in her. Why these sudden blotches on the face, the threads of gray hair, and worst of all, the deep fleshy rings encircling her neck like Indian bangles—dozens of them!

"Look at you!" Mr. Adewale exclaims, seeing how his daughter is dressed. "Who told you to dress like Jezebel?

"Go and change!" chimes Mrs. Adewale.

"Didn't you hear your mother? Go and change!"

"She's not my mother," Tinuke mutters, seething at being shamed in front of the wicked witch.

"Go!" he shouts, loud enough for Cecilia to hear from the kitchen.

Cecilia lifts the frying pan off the stove and listens. She's worked for this family long enough to know when to be quiet, but now that she's decided to leave, she wonders why she bothers. She thinks again of the petroleum minister whose cook, the papers say, stole millions from the minister's vault. What she intends to take is just pocket change in comparison.

"Cecilia!" Mr. Adewale calls.

"Saaah." Cecilia hastily dries her hands against her apron and hurries to the breakfast room, straightening and pulling down her skirt as she goes.

"Where are my eggs?"

"Is coming, sah!"

"And toast? What's taking you so long? Hurry up!" He claps his hands quickly.

"Sorry, sah. I'm coming just now."

Cecilia scurries back to the kitchen, relights the burner, and starts frying the onions. She pauses for a moment, listening to make sure nobody's coming, then spits into the bowl of eggs. She beats swiftly before pouring the eggs into the pan. While the omelet cooks, she serves the akara and cuts the toast into triangles. When everything is ready, she wipes her brow with two fingers and flicks the sweat onto her employer's plate. Added seasoning for his coming up behind her yesterday and squeezing her breasts while she was removing a cake from the oven. She ought to have thrown the hot pan at his feet.

Mr. and Mrs. sit silently over the remains of breakfast. Beneath the table, Mrs. Adewale fingers the unwanted bulges that pad her waist, and with her other hand helps herself to a third piece of toast, regardless. Mr. Adewale momentarily returns to thoughts of his neighbors before drifting back to more pleasant thoughts of his current love—Nadia.

Upstairs in her bedroom, Tinuke throws herself onto her bed, and with muffled cries pounds the mattress with both fists. "I can't take it, can't take it!" she sobs, eventually sitting up. She unzips her jeans, flings them to one side and puts on a skirt, wipes the tears from her face, and stares at her seventeen-year-old self in the mirror. *Just a few more weeks,* she reminds herself. *Just a few more weeks.*

Mr. Adewale eyes his daughter, now back at the breakfast table, dressed in more sensible clothing. He reaches over to squeeze her shoulder, but she pulls away. Let her be then. He remembers her as a little girl, the way she used to sit on his lap and eat from his plate. He used to carry her around on his shoulders, play tickling games, and tell ijapa tales of the clever tortoise outwitting all the other animals of the forest. The stories made her laugh, and for a while she took to calling herself Ijapa, hiding behind furniture and then jumping out to shout, *Boo!* Not anymore though. Now she seems wary of him. Accuses him of being too strict. But if you were to see her ample breasts and the way her buttocks move so seductively in tight jeans . . . He sucks his teeth.

Everyone in the Adewale household understands that when it's time for Mr. Adewale's swimming lesson, they're not allowed to watch, so they do. The gardeners peep through the purple bougainvillea by the side of the house, while Cecilia watches from the conservatory. They see him looking silly in his knee-length shorts tied with a drawstring that disappears beneath a bulging stomach. They watch as he lowers himself gingerly into the water, holding onto the handrails as though his life depends on it, until both feet are firmly planted in the shallow end. The water cuts him off below the chest, and he stands for some moments with arms held high above the water, shaking as he eyes the pool's inflatable life buoy for reassurance. The gardeners laugh at the sight of the boss looking foolish, although it's Nadia who interests them the most. When she stands in the shallow end, water glistens like jewels on her bare shoulders and swishes around her waist beneath her large breasts. The workers have heard that the latter may not be real, that Master may have paid for them to be just so. People with money can afford such things. Her skin is light and even lighter in places normally covered by clothes. When she swims, her long brown hair fans out behind her. She allows Master to cling to the edge and tells him to kick, but he has trouble with this maneuver and the goddess must hold him stable under his tummy. The gardeners laugh again, imagining what must be happening down there in the aquamarine pool. Cecilia looks on with disgust while Mrs. Adewale, herself a former mistress, observes in anger from the balcony of the upstairs bedroom.

Tinuke is the only one not watching her father flail

around in the water. She's messaged a friend, changed back into jeans and a halter top, and sneaked away. Sami waits for her outside the front gate in his father's Range Rover. They drive to the Eko Hotel where Sami buys drinks and they sit outside beneath a parasol. They chat, but mostly just smoke while Tinuke stares at the pool. "Wish they'd both drown," she mutters, thinking of her father and his latest girlfriend.

"Forget about them," Sami says, standing up. "At least you'll soon be back at boarding school, at least your father has the money to send you away!"

"I don't care about his money," she snaps, wishing Sami didn't have to bring everything back to money.

"Look, we've been here for hours, let's go to the beach," he suggests, trying to cheer her up.

"Not now." She sighs, standing up. "Shit!" she whispers.

"What?"

Tinuke indicates with a jerk of her head.

"Shit," Sami mumbles, turning to see the fat man striding toward them. Mr. Adewale glares angrily at the table with the bottles of beer, the half-eaten suya, and the empty pack of Marlboro Lights.

"Get out!" he shouts.

Sami backs away, but not before Mr. Adewale grabs him by the shirt and slaps him. Sami yelps in pain.

"Daddy!" Tinuke screams, wishing her friend wasn't such a wimp, such a little boy.

Mr. Adewale takes his daughter and marches her past the hotel guests, back to his car. The driver, thinking he and the radio were all there would be for the next few hours, is dozing when Mr. Adewale arrives and flings his daughter across the backseat. In his rage, Mr. Adewale forgets that he's brought Nadia to the hotel and left her waiting by the bar.

"Never," he shouts at Tinuke, "will I see you with any stupid boys again, behaving like a tramp and a whore! And from now on, there's no more going out! You hear? You hear?"

"Leave me!" she cries.

"Did you fuck him?" he shouts.

The driver glances in his rearview mirror, his eyes widening at the look of fury on the girl's face as she leans forward. What he doesn't see is how hard she's squeezing her legs, her hands futile against her father's hand, thrust between her thighs.

Back at the house, Mr. Adewale storms past the gardeners and the security guards who look away sheepishly, knowing they too will suffer for this.

"Leave me alone! Stop dragging me!" Tinuke screams, wriggling from her father's grip.

"Come back!" he shouts, as Tinuke runs, clutching her face where he's just slapped her. "Go outside and clean the pool. From now on you'll stay at home. No going out and no returning to England! No more boarding school for you. You're staying here, where I can keep my eye on you."

"No way, I'm not staying!" Tinuke screams, running to her room and locking the door behind her.

An hour later, the house is quiet. Mr. Adewale, barely able to stand after the afternoon's exertions, lies down. Mrs. Adewale watches him as he starts to snore, kisses her teeth in disgust, then returns to thoughts of what to wear for the evening prayer meeting. She cannot decide what is most likely to impress her new pastor. Straight-laced or seductive? Cheap or expensive? The church has just launched its sacrifice drive, requesting congregants to give at their highest level—in naira, dollars, pounds, or euros. Failing that, people can donate their cars, houses, or land. And seeing that she has helped the pastor redesign the pledge forms, she knows she must be careful not to dress too flamboyantly.

Mr. Adewale stirs. He sits up, still complaining of a headache. Mrs. Adewale sighs, goes to the bathroom, opens the medicine cabinet, and takes out some pills. "Here, dear," she says, offering him more than he needs. He throws them back quickly, almost chocking on one before he stands up and waddles over to the window. "Careful," she calls, guessing that the reason he races out has something to do with what he must have spotted his neighbors doing outside. But she has better things to do than fuss over him. She must dress for tonight and find out what that girl Cecilia is up to.

Cecilia is downstairs chopping plantains and wondering when Tinuke might reappear. She's never seen so much anger on a child's face. She heats her oil and starts frying the perfectly sliced yellow circles of which she is most proud, using a fork to turn them when they are golden. By next week, God willing, she'll have other maids working for her. And all she'll do is fry plantains and polish silver. But then, what is she thinking? If all goes according to plan, she'll never have to work again. She forgets about Tinuke until she hears someone shouting and runs out to see what's happening. Master is racing down the stairs, shirt undone. He opens the sliding doors that lead to the pool, and there is Tinuke, dressed in a red bikini, smoking.

"Tinuke!" Cecilia calls out in warning, seeing that the girl is wearing headphones and her eyes are closed. The father cannot abide cigarettes.

Seemingly unaware of who has just arrived, Tinuke dips a foot into the deep end and nonchalantly splashes water. *Try me*, she's thinking, *just try me*, as her father rushes toward her.

"What are you wearing?" he shouts, snatching roughly at the strap of her bikini top. Tinuke's hand moves as if to cover the exposed breast, only to lash out instead, striking him hard across his neck. Cecilia sees it all. One leg goes up, the other follows, and then he falls, banging his head on the concrete as he lands. For one uncertain moment, the head lolls back over the edge of the pool, and the shoulders follow, and then with a rapid whoosh and a half-hearted splash, all of him slips in and under. Tinuke throws the butt of her cigarette into the water after him. She waits for a minute, then another. Then she screams for help.

WHAT ARE YOU GOING TO DO?

BY ADEBOLA RAYO

Onikan

When the traffic inches forward, I watch as the wheel cover on the car ahead of me moves, jutting out ever so slightly and spinning almost independently of the wheel. For a brief moment, I imagine it flying off, cutting through my windscreen, and slicing my head down the middle. I hold onto that image, thinking it would be an interesting way to die. I only wonder if it would be painless, if I'd be dead before I realized what happened.

I imagine that the last thing I would see is the wheel cover hurtling through the air, and that I'd be shocked and fascinated by the horror of it, not knowing that it was coming for me. Would I die immediately, or would my head, split in two in the last moments of consciousness, recognize that my eyes were seeing from farther apart than usual?

The traffic is starting to build up. I knew it would if I left work this late, but my attempt to leave at five p.m. on the dot was thwarted when my boss dropped a folder on my desk at a quarter to five and sat on my table. I hated it when he did that. What was it about me that made him feel comfortable enough to plop himself on my desk? And why did he like these last-minute tasks so much? I was convinced he did it on purpose, deriving some sort of satisfaction from making me stay back. Knowing that, unlike my colleagues, I wouldn't try to convince him to let me turn it in in the morning.

So, at 6:33 p.m. I find myself pulling into the traffic in front of the marina next to the governor's residence. Sometimes I want to park my car and just go sit by the sea. But these government dunderheads have put up fences around the parks and waterfront. And besides, there's nowhere to park. I miss water. I miss sitting on the sand at Bar Beach with the smell and smoke of Igbo teasing me as the boys on the beach smoke joints. They filled the ocean with sand to build their Atlantic City, can you imagine that? These government people won't let us have anything, even moments of quiet.

But what's the point of getting angry in a city like Lagos, where everything tries to drive you up the wall? You will just kill yourself for nothing, as my boss likes to say. Though I shouldn't be quoting that motherfucker because I'm pissed. But again, what's the point of getting angry? It's not like I can easily find a new job if I quit this one.

"Ashewo, o je lo gba driver. Who gave you car?"

I don't even realize these words are directed at me until the yellow taxi pulls up so close to my car that I could lean over the passenger's side and touch his wrinkling, tribal-marked face if I wanted to. I watch him gesture about my driving skills for a few more seconds.

"All you small, small girls with the car your aristo sugar daddy bought you."

I roll up the windows and turn on the AC. I stare at the dents and the chipped yellow paint of his old Toyota. I can see him laughing and gesturing at me intermittently, even as he drives forward. I still don't know what I have done to annoy this man. When the car ahead of me moves, I drive till I draw up to the yellow taxi and swerve my car into his. I hear the screech of tires as the car behind stops short of my bumper, but I barely pay attention. I watch the taxi driver's jaw drop then begin to move furiously as he curses at me. I turn my music up. He is still struggling with his door when the car behind me reverses and pulls out into the next lane. I turn the wheel, reverse, and drive off. In my rearview mirror, I watch as the gray-bearded man continues to struggle with his car door.

Stephanie is at my door—not at the gate, at the door. I hand my car key to the guard, making a mental note to scold him for letting her in. He should know better than to let anyone enter without my permission.

"The mechanic will come and pick up the car early in the morning. Don't wake me," I say to him.

Since I started working at the microfinance bank two years ago, Stephanie and I have only had a reason to talk twice: the two times my boss wanted me to request a bribe from applicants before he approved their loans. I'd gone to her both times because she was in HR. Both conversations went the same way.

I'd say, "This isn't a part of my job description, and I thought I should report Kaz to HR because I don't want to do this."

Her laugh, like a bird's shrill caw, was loud and sharp. It sounded like a weird mating call. "Tola, everybody does it. Just explain to the applicant that it will speed up the process."

Both times I caved and, without protest, kept the N50,000 my boss left on my table the morning after he approved the loans. The money was useful, anyway. There's no point getting angry or acting stupid here in Lagos.

"Sorry I showed up at your door like this," Stephanie says. She is staring at me in a way that lets me know I have my resting-bitch face on again.

"It's okay," I reply, even though we both know it's not.

I open the door to my apartment. "I have a pet, so don't scream."

"Because of a dog?" She laughs nervously as she walks in. I turn on the light and she lets out a half-scream before composing herself. She giggles again and moves closer to the wall opposite the glass cage.

"It's in a cage," I say. I imagine that the dead mouse in there probably made Lucy look scarier. "She's slow these days; I don't know why she hasn't had her breakfast."

The shrill nervous laugh comes again. I wonder what she'd do if I told her Lucy tried to bite me twice in the last week while I was cleaning.

Every woman has that friend—you know, the one you go to when you need a procedure done. You don't go to her because she told you she's had one done, you go to her because you *know* she has.

After five minutes of beating around the bush, wondering if you should say you're asking on behalf of a friend, you come right out and say it: "I'm pregnant, and I need to find somewhere to get rid of it."

You hold her stare, and your eyes beg her not to pretend that she doesn't know a place, that she hasn't had a procedure.

Less than a year later, here I am being ambushed into being that friend for Stephanie. I'd never told her I'd had an abortion, but I figure she must have not believed it was typhoid that caused me to constantly walk briskly into the ladies' room for two weeks. Especially since I'd refused to go to the office clinic, saying it would pass. It did pass, after I took two personal days off and came back looking as normal as ever.

I'm so hungry for a smoke that after frantically searching my hollowed-out decorative book, I go to my ashtray and light a quarter-smoked joint I find there.

All the while she's watching me without a word. I recognize the look in her eyes.

"Don't worry, I don't feel the need to hide certain things about myself," I say.

Stephanie spends the next two hours crying and telling me about her issues with the man she's dating. I spend the time relighting partially smoked joints. I drag on about six of them till my fingers are burning.

"You just have to learn how to pleasure yourself by yourself," I mutter.

"What?"

"I have to let Lucy out soon," I say.

She starts to leave a few minutes later—without a phone number, but with detailed directions to the clinic.

"It's been there for about fifteen years, my friend told me. You'll find it easily."

She pauses and asks what I think the likelihood of a police raid is.

I laugh. "In Nigeria?"

"You should laugh more. Or smile." She is standing at the door, inviting mosquitoes into my house, talking this nonsense. "People in the office say you never smile, and when you do it is fake because your eyes look dead. Your laughter sounds nice. A little scary, but nice."

Later that night, I stand in my bathroom naked, smiling at my reflection. With teeth showing. Without. With lips spread wide. Without. Only left cheek raised. I smile. Eyes widened. Eyes crinkled. I smile.

Some days, like today, I get really tired. I want to be at home with the covers over my head but I'm sitting at my desk instead, earphones in, Frank Ocean's "Strawberry Swing" playing so loudly it is going to my chest. I'm watching the others at their desks in the open office, looking like bubbleheads. They're loud bubbleheads, and I really want to scream at everyone to shut the fuck up and get out. Days like this, I hate people. Hate their ease of conversation, their laughter, their being.

I walk to the bathroom and call my doctor to ask if it's okay that I've been using diazepam to sleep, along with the prescribed epilim.

"I should have told you before I started taking it, but it's just been hard to sleep and every night I try on my own but it's been impossible."

"Try it for two more days and if you still can't sleep, we'll find you something to use more permanently."

"Okay," I say. "Also, I'm running out of diazepam."

"Have you been drinking coffee?"

"Yes, in the mornings."

"You know you are not allowed that. It's a stimulant."

I whine about how he's taking all the good things in my life away from me. We always do this: I complain about every drug and instruction; he insists I do what is best for me.

"Something is bothering you. That's why you can't sleep and that's why you're cranky."

"It's nothing."

Honestly, it *is* nothing. Sometimes this happens. I don't know there is something, but I'm reacting to it, then I finally figure out what it is hours or days later.

"All of this sucks."

"What?"

"Living. It gets heavy after a while."

"Have you thought more about taking a vacation?"

"See, the only reason I like to go to new places is because I like the journey, eating up roads or clouds and moving through the world quickly—it's just the way I want to live: a flash through life. I wish journeys would last forever. Like I wonder if the plane could just keep flying and never land. So I don't have to actually live, work, or vacation. I like sitting in a plane or a car with nothing to do but just watch time pass."

"You know you could make your life a constant journey, right? Be an air hostess or something," he says.

"No, no. Then I'd be living during the journey. Serving people. I hate interacting with people."

"Okay."

He says nothing else for a while and I think the connection has broken. Then, "So, why do you like suspending your life?"

This is the part I hate. Whatever answer I give won't satisfy him. He'll try to find some deeper meaning to it and ask me if that's what I'm masking. That's why I prefer the phone calls, because it's easier to get out of the conversations.

I shake my head. "I don't know."

I hear that little *ah* sound, but the silence fills the space again, like when someone starts to say something but they change their mind. I hated it when my last boyfriend did that. To have my therapist do the same thing is even more annoying.

"That's your assignment," he says after a while. "Write about why you want to suspend living."

"But I already wrote about why I want to die."

"So, is the answer to both the same?"

I think for a moment. "No," I reply.

"If you say no, that means you already know the answer. But I won't push. We'll talk about it in our next session, okay? Actually, you need to come in person soon."

"Okay."

On my way back to my desk, I walk past Kaz's office and he calls out for a cup of coffee.

I used to get angry about being asked to perform these menial tasks, but not anymore. I stop at my desk to pick up my purse. Then I make him a cup of coffee. What's the point of getting angry in this Lagos? I add two cubes of sugar, and two ten-milligram diazepam tablets. No cream. I started adding the tablets last week after his wife came in to drop off his hypotension medication one morning. He didn't notice when I added one pill; he still hasn't noticed now that I use two.

After work, I walk past Freedom Park, turn left on Broad Street, and head to the taxi park in front of the hospital. I stop at the makeshift canteen, where a group of men are sitting under a sign that says, *No idle sitting—eat your food and go.*

"I'm going to Lekki."

One of them gets up and says, "N3,500, let's go."

"E never reach your turn-o." He yells back that Baba Hafusa has gone to pray, so it's his turn. The other men grumble and argue.

"Is anyone going?" I ask, tired of their bickering.

"See," one pipes up, "Baba Hafusa ti n bo."

The man who wanted N3,500 says to me, "Sorry, sister, the next person has come."

I turn around and see a limping man. I reach into my mind, trying to figure out why he looks so familiar.

"Sister, where are you going? My car is in front."

I walk behind him. "Lekki, and I'm only paying N3,000. Will you drive . . ." I drift off as he lays a hand on his bonnet, rubbing the chipped yellow paint on its dent.

"N3,500, aunty. Traffic go plenty at this time. Where is the address?"

So I sit in the back, listening to the engine rattle and the sound of him hacking up phlegm between coughs, and I wonder if he recognized me too. Probably not, because he's chattering away about the traffic and the new fuel price, and for the first time I'm happy that I chose to pay the police for a car tint permit that was supposed to be free.

"Now I have to work nights because of this fuel increase," he's saying. "Good thing I finished praying and saw you. After evening prayers now I carry one more passenger, then I go home to Iya Hafusa."

I don't know what it is about me that invites monologues from stangers, but there's no point getting angry or saying I don't want to talk. I just nod, *hmm*, and *eeyah* from time to time.

I'm leaning back so the chair is rocking on its hind legs. He flips through my file and then stares at the prescription pad.

"Are you sleeping these days?"

"Not without the diazepam."

"Did you try breaking the pills in half like I told you to?"

"No."

"What about the dreams?"

"They're still there. Very vivid."

"Still sci-fi themed?"

"Yes, and I still wake with a heavy head."

The nurse smiles when she sees me on my way out. "You're adding some weight. That's very good."

I smile back at her, but as soon as I get outside I turn to look at my reflection in the glass door. I've put on three kilos since I started using epilim, that's three kilos more than I've gained in the last ten years, since I hit my last growth spurt at fourteen. I know I'll obsess about it again but I tell myself not to panic.

I go to the canteen to eat amala and ewedu before heading to the pharmacy. I've developed a rhythm around my visits and I have to do everything in the same order. The last time I came, there was no ewedu soup and I found myself tearing up later at the pharmacy.

Today, to make up for that last time, I order an extra portion and tell my past self that everything will be all right at the end of the day.

I hate waiting, but I find that often I have to wait for others to arrive. So now I'm sitting here nursing a lukewarm bottle of Coke, waiting for the taxi driver to get here. I hate driving to the mainland, but that's not why I'm waiting for him. I've been driving less and less these days, and finding myself at the taxi stand more often. Some days they say he's out, but I wait for him to come back and drive me home from work. Today, I took a taxi to Yaba from home, then I called and told him to meet me here at three p.m. Yet now it's 3:32 and I'm still waiting.

Lucy has barely been eating for weeks, and I'm tired of my apartment smelling like dead mice. I moved her cage to the spare bedroom two weeks ago, but I can't avoid taking her to the vet anymore. I put her in the shift box and latch it.

At work, whenever anyone asks me what's inside the box, I say that it's toys for my nephews.

"I didn't know you had nephews," Kaz says, grinding his hips into my desk and shifting my papers to make space for himself. "In fact, I thought you were an only child."

"Yeah." The box shakes and I raise my voice: "There are rattles in there. I should take out the batteries."

"Have lunch with me today," Kaz says. "You play hard to get."

I smile.

"You see? I've never seen you smile. Your eyes are prettier when you smile."

"I have to run a quick errand to VI at lunch," I say, pointing at the box. "Is it okay if I go?"

"Okay, but you can't escape me. Clear it with HR and go. You must have lunch with me soon, Tola. But before you go, please make me some coffee."

I smile and widen my eyes as he walks out.

I go to the kitchen to make him a cup of coffee. Three cubes of sugar this time, with eight ten-milligram diazepam tablets and no cream.

When I give it to him, he looks at me and says, "When you come back, please remind me to call my doctor. The man says my drugs haven't been working well."

"It must be all the coffee you drink," I remark.

"Hey, Steph." I drop by her office before my lunch break. These days I call her Steph—it makes her eager to do what I want. She smiles. Her smile is pretty, unlike her laugh.

"What's up, girl?"

I tell myself not to cringe, so I smile and widen my eyes. I've learned that it makes my eyes brighter and my smile seem more genuine.

"I have to run a quick errand and I don't know how long it'll take. Cover for me?"

"Sure, girl."

"You're the best."

I hold the shift box in front of me and walk to the taxi stand on Broad Street. All the cabbies know me by this point.

"Baba Hafusa," one of them calls out, "come and carry your customer-o."

But he's busy arguing in front of the hospital gate. The young lady he's talking to has a phone in her hand and is not paying him mind.

"I be taxi driver nor mean say I nor fit born you. I get your type at home. I have child your age. Mo ni e nile nau."

"Oga, story niyen, please give me my change."

And this is the point where he flips and threatens to slap her.

"Try it," she says, typing on her phone.

"What are you going to do?" he yells at her.

The other men are laughing and telling him to leave her alone.

"You get customer wey dey wait for you-o," the taxi park chairman calls out to him.

The driver sees me and walks over. "Don't mind this Ashewo girl," he says. "All these small, small girls are following big men, and because of that she thinks she can be talking rude to me."

I stare at him, willing him to shut up. My phone beeps. It's a message from Stephanie: *Babes! Kaz just collapsed in the office. They're taking him to the hospital. Poor guy.*

I smile and my eyes widen.

"All these Lagos girls," the taxi driver says as he jimmies open his door. "You close early?"

I get in the back. "No, I'm going to VI."

As he turns onto Marina Road, I say to him, "Did you know that girl you were fighting with?"

"No-o. I drove the yeye girl to the hospital and she's talking rude because of N200."

"So why did you call her a prostitute?"

"All these Lagos girls, that's what they are," he replies. "God save us from them. Few responsible girls with job like you."

I smile. "But why must woman exist for man to be closer to God?"

"What? I don't understand."

"I guess man always needs a woman to blame." I twist the latch on Lucy's shift box and let her slither onto my lap and down my legs.

"Are you talking to me, aunty?"

"Stop at the beginning of Ahmadu Bello," I tell him, handing him money.

"I go carry you home for evening?"

"We'll see," I say, clutching the empty box to my chest.

FOR BABY, FOR THREE

BY ONYINYE IHEZUKWU

Yaba

Right there, at the street corner by the roundabout that circumscribed the faded statue of the army general in a marshaling pose, stood Bisola's food shed. It was an old shed, built from corrugated zinc, cardboard flaps, and an oversized sun umbrella to protect her burning coal embers from the frequent lashes of gritty breeze. Bisola's Power Joint, everyone called it—for it was here you could buy the best roasted corn and coconuts, when in season, or the juiciest chicken gizzards dunked in pepper sauce and garnished with onion rings. Even better—this was like legend—her akara was made from properly processed, unadulterated bean paste fried in properly purchased, unadulterated vegetable oil. When the bean balls emerged from her pan of hot oil, they remained golden brown with a soft simmering dent in the middle, so abounding with freshness that people lined up for meters to fill their stomachs with these spheres of delight. For her regular customers, Bisola dusted a spice mixture of pepper and groundnuts into the dents in the center, then smiled a dimpled smile when the non-regulars protested the unfairness of her selective service. Pretending to point out that the added spice would cost them more, she would sprinkle the pepper and groundnuts anyway, talking in her slurred, deep voice and working her large, veiny hands. Her laugh sounded like a drum roll from the marching drill at the army barracks not far away, a laugh that might have tumbled from something strong, like the chest of the statue of the army general perpetually striding toward her shed, observing her as she sat basting gizzards, roasting corn, and molding bean cakes six days a week from noon till a little after ten p.m.

Now a buyer was requesting two particularly large corn cobs, evenly browned on all sides from where they lay on the coal wire mesh. Bisola quickly plucked them off the mesh in swift motions, blowing on her fingers to soothe the sting. She bent over to rip a page off a heap of newspapers in the corner, and as she wrapped the steaming cobs in the paper, the customer said, "You're forgetting the coconuts, na."

Bisola tapped her waist and thumped her chest softly. She blinked. "Sorry," she replied, and leaned over, cradling her stomach to reach the basin of shelled coconuts.

"Ah, this belly issue is getting in the way," the buyer said with a grin. "Since this belly, Bisola has been forgetting, na."

The other customers laughed. One woman piped up: "And you people think carrying baby is easy? God should have made you men share in the work too. Then we'll see who'll cry first."

A man not far away scoffed. "Huh? What is there to cry about? Baby business? You mean making baby? But that's easiest of all!"

Bisola, with a face flushed from the heat of her ashes and a chest filled with the acid of her badly digested lunch, did not flash her dimples this time at the teasing. She let them talk, trying to ignore the sensations of stiffness in her shoulders, peering above the customers' heads as if searching for something in the horizon. Her mind held a ticking clock inside. This moment—the sun setting over the barracks, the young children peddling biscuits and wristwatches, the motorcycle riders fleeing annoyed traffic wardens—all pointed to the fact that it was about six p.m., offices were closed, the prayer meeting was at hand, and Osei would be arriving soon to pick her up.

She watched the signs, marking the bustling world through the fumes rising from her pan of oil.

When the last batch of akara was served up, she refused to mix a new batter. She sprinkled water on the coals and slowly rose to her feet. The customers in line raised a fuming chorus. She said, as quietly as she could, "I don close. Come back tomorrow." Then she uprooted the sun umbrella from the soft earth and folded it like a pocketknife. Through the threats of departing customers, none of which she responded to, she gathered her wares of business: the glass showcase for fried gizzards, the now-empty basin for holding coconuts preserved in water, the wire mesh, raffia fan, sitting stool, coal pot, batter pot, and plastic spice containers; and stacked these items inside the slanted shed of zinc and cardboard. She sat on the stool inside, pulling the door slightly closed so she could still see Osei arrive. She stretched her long, trunk-sized legs before her, huffing and belching and thumping her chest softly.

Twice she leaned forward to peer through the door at the sound of an approaching motorcycle, and then she stepped outside to study the roads carefully. It was darker now, the sun had set completely, leaving a faint yellow cast on the general's face of stone. His boots, surrounded here and there by dogs plodding among small patches of grass, held her attention for a moment before she remembered that she didn't want to be seen by persistent customers thinking she had changed her mind. She watched the roundabout again, noticing a traffic warden blowing a whistle and charging at a ducking and laughing motorcycle man; a child hawking Coke ran after a motorist for his money; and a distant bugle blared from the barracks. The prayer meeting was at six thirty. Now traffic was almost locked. Did Osei not leave his shop in time?

She retreated to the shed and checked the collection of gifts again. She could tell, from placing her hands around the food warmer, that the specially reserved akara balls were still hot, along with the gizzards in the saucer inside the warmer. There was a bundle of three yams tied together with a string. And there was the broiler chicken, now too tired to squawk, lying quietly on its side and blinking in the dimness of the shed. Bisola turned to the door, her face pressed to the rotting zinc. Osei had not left his shop in time.

When the rattling combustion sounds of his motorcycle finally drew near, she was on her feet to greet him. He hurried in like there was a secret he had been rushing to say, but just as the putrid air of the chicken's shit hit his nose, he stopped and rubbed his goatee. He turned to his wife, who was watching him from her towering height.

"Bisi," he said.

"We're late, my husband."

Osei rubbed his forehead. He smelled like the orange air freshener that hung above his barbershop mirror. He stroked his goatee again, then examined his fingernails. His delicate lips moved as if to kiss something in the air. Then he was saying, "The customers, today's business . . ."

"I have the money for the pastor. It's all right."

Osei nodded, but did not look up.

Bisola motioned to the stool. "Sit."

He lowered himself carefully onto the stool, his legs pressed together like a girl's. He polished off his dinner as soon as Bisola served it, and while she put the empty plates away, he found a tortoiseshell comb in his breast pocket and brushed his hair in three quick strokes: one each for the flat sides along his ears and another for the well-greased punk outgrowth in the middle. He rose to his feet and his eyes smiled. "Look at this stinking shit. But what has this chicken been eating all day! Your roasted corn, eh?"

"Take the yams and the food," Bisola replied. "I'll carry the chicken."

Osei flexed his shoulders, cracked his fingers. "I feel alive!"

Bisola picked up the now-clucking chicken. As she found a string to tie its feet together, Osei said, "What if I grabbed these volleyballs the way you're grabbing that chicken?" He took hold of her ample behind, one throbbing cheek in each palm. He wriggled them around in her cotton dress. "Jigi-jigi! Look at that!"

Bisola tapped her chest, trying to hold down a belch.

"And the ball in front!" Osei rubbed her stomach, cackling loudly.

Bisola opened the squeaky door and stepped into the night. Osei followed her, still talking, and after he watched her secure the chicken to the back carrier of his motorcycle, he remembered he had left his keys inside the shed. When he reappeared a moment later with keys in hand, he was quiet, his lips puckered and contemplating. Bisola climbed into the backseat, securing the machine with her weight so he could get on with ease. She angled her frame so that Osei's elbows would not bump against her stomach. As he started the ignition, she asked in a soft voice, "You think baby can feel your hand now?"

He paused. "My child. My own child." He pumped the cycle's pedal with a small foot. "When the pastor brings it back to life."

Osei zoomed in the direction of the roundabout.

* * *

The pastor with the long name—Joshua Isefudiah Promise Esoko Loveday—was no ordinary pastor, like the ones used for headaches and small fevers. It was known that his name, meandering as it was, was that way because an angel had bestowed it on him in the nine minutes the man, while yet unconverted, had died in a drinking parlor, gone to hell, then heaven, and back to earth. To consolidate his mission, the pastor received what he said was a designation of numbers from the angel. It didn't matter what the problem was; there was a fixed length of time in heaven for every problem on earth. The angel broke down the numbers to him in a prehistoric code, one that had existed since languages evolved from Babel of Bible times. First the pastor would lay a hand on a believer's head, determine the root cause, and the number of hours, days, or months needed to pray till it was all over.

Bisola's was three thousand years, reduced to three days, because the pastor said that with God, a day was like a thousand years. And three was a figure that held the power of resurrection, since Jesus lay in the tomb three days and three nights. Three sessions of prayer over three days and the dead would be restored to life. Two done and one left. This was what Bisola's ticking clock indicated as she was pulled on her husband's motorcycle, through the dust gathering on her thick calves, along thirteen kilometers of traffic on the bridge off the mainland of Lagos, till they found themselves in the fishing settlements. The houses started passing as soon as they came off the bridge, slowly pulling into Yaba where a fork appeared in the main street, leading the way to the defunct plastic factory. Behind the factory was a complex of administrative offices, long and curving slightly. The offices stretched side by side for kilometers, but the pastor had claimed only a few, along with the reception lobby which could seat close to a hundred people.

Bisola and Osei could not find a seat when they walked in. The ticket taker was in her usual place: on a narrow stage of mounted bricks, seated behind a table that overlooked the rest of the hall where people sat in clusters according to appointment times. Those who had no seats wandered about calling out for family, suckled babies, or snored on mats in corners. Peace enforcers, recruited from the pastor's own church disciples, shouted here and there for order. One threatened a crying toddler. Another enforcer carried a standing fan in search of a place to set it down. The heat was choking.

Bisola pressed to the front, pulling Osei behind her. She showed her ticket to the woman on stage and the woman frowned without looking up. "No, no. You're late. You'll have to wait, na."

"But I'm—"

The woman looked up. "See," she pointed at a group, "those are seven forty-five people. They are next."

Bisola said, "I'm pregnant."

The woman looked Bisola up and down. She called to an enforcer and whispered into his ear. The man went away and returned with a high-backed plastic chair. The ticket woman handed it to Bisola. "Sit down. Find a place and sit down."

With chair in one hand and the squawking chicken in the other, Bisola caught the attention of a thin-lipped, petite woman who turned to move her sleeping son's body on the floor. Bisola thanked her and set down the chair, then placed the chicken beneath it. When she turned to Osei to receive the other thanksgiving items, she saw that he was looking again at his fingernails. His face was flushed from the heat, his hair grease running along his ears.

Bisola took the items and placed them under the chair. "Sit." She stood to the side and Osei fell into the chair, his knees neatly pushed together. The thin-lipped woman stared, openmouthed, and Bisola spoke calmly: "He's not well. My good husband is not well."

An enforcer with an old microphone and speaker horn was calling for the next batch, the seven forty-five. All around, people stirred afresh, falling into line, searching for drifting children and spouses. Bisola immediately seized an empty chair just as a man was making his way toward it. The man cried, "Even the one with a big stomach is strong enough to seize my blessings!" and looked around frantically for another seat. He advanced as soon as he saw one, but then stopped and made another exclamation. Bisola sat a short distance from Osei since there was no space beside him. She wedged the hem of her dress between her spread knees, leaned forward to massage her swollen ankles with the heel of her hand. Positioned like that, with her back slightly bent and face angled to the right, she could smell Osei's oranges across the distance between them, a fragrance undaunted by the dust and exhaust smoke of travel, or the fumes of cooking coals and sulphuric belches trapped in her clothes. He was studying the crowd around him with a detached gaze, his slender fingers going *tap, tap, tap* in his lap. Soon, she knew, he would say he was going out for fresh air; and fresh air would take time, whatever length of time it took for her to move through the line, wait at the inner anteroom, and have the pastor finally minister to her and her baby in his office.

She kept up the pressure on her ankle, waiting for Osei to make his exit, waiting for the enforcer with the microphone and speaker to announce a new group with her added to it. The enforcer made a new announcement after about an hour, and when she joined in and he demanded to see her ticket, she said she was six thirty. The enforcer paused a moment, then waved her on. Bisola turned to Osei, who passed her the chicken and yams. Seeing she was overloaded, he held onto the flask of food.

"I'm going for some fresh air," he said. "I'll bring the food when I return."

Bisola hesitated.

"Just a little fresh air," he said. "Just a little fresh air."

His lips were doing the movement again. Bisola turned and followed the group, trudging carefully to avoid collisions with the bodies pressing around her. A corridor stretched from the reception lobby to the pastor's converted offices, its floor of ceramic tiles disintegrating to show the mossy concrete beneath. Slowed by the gas scorching its way about her chest, the offering items in both her hands, and the growing worry that now Osei should come back to join in the prayers, she found herself left behind as others pushed on.

For the first time since she'd walked down this corridor two days ago, she took the time to observe the framed Bible verses along the walls. People said that when K. Kasamu, the oil magnate, still ran the factory as a front for his friend and then-president, you could see huge framed portraits of Kasamu and the army general on the walls and in every office. But the pictures were all gone; it was now fifteen years since the general had fallen from power and Kasamu had fled the country. In those days, the people on television said he had been airlifted to the Cameroonian border, where he made his way to Europe disguised as a woman. *As if being a woman would make escape any easier,* Bisola thought. She studied the framed verses that stretched beside her on both sides now, squinting to read them. She slowly called out the numbers under her breath: "*Five . . . one . . . twenty-two . . .*" Numbers were more familiar, being articles she dealt with daily in her trade. As for the words, she tried to string them together if a familiar vowel was present. There was *Lord, Hope, Je-sus, Se-vy-you* or *Say-vee-yor.* Yes, *Savior.* Osei had pointed out that word to her once. She felt a headache coming and looked away from the walls.

Bisola stepped into the anteroom where fewer people sat in chairs arranged in rows. This room led to the pastor's main office where he met one-on-one with supplicants. Bisola found a seat, right beside the family that had been ahead of her, once again placing the chicken and yams on the floor. There was a lady enforcer seated not far from the pastor's door, ushering people into the office in turns. When someone stepped out, the enforcer waved her hand at the waiting group. The next person rose and walked into the office, while the rest of the group migrated up the chairs, shuffling quietly. Sounds intermittently boomed through the door: that of the pastor's voice broken by the crazed scream of a supplicant, or a chorus of clapping and singing. And when crashes and clatters could be heard inside, everyone in the anteroom understood it was the pastor chasing the evil spirit around the office.

Bisola patiently moved up the seats, pulling the chicken and yams along as she went. As she settled into a new chair, warm from the body heat of the person who'd just vacated it, she placed a hand on her stomach and said a prayer: "Baby will live again on the third day. Baby is alive."

These were the exact words the pastor had told her to say three times a day for three days. Today was the third day; this was her second repetition today. The third and final time she would say it would be in the office, right there with the pastor's final act of resurrection. It was going to be great, she could feel it. The gas hadn't receded; it burned as strongly as it had when baby was still kicking, which was a sign that there was still life inside her. Those hospital people would say she told them so. Her baby's heart was still working, its mouth yawning, its eyes blinking. Those machines could make mistakes. They used batteries, didn't they?

The way Osei had explained it to her, the machine—with the screen and the other part that looked like a corn cob—worked like a telephone, except it wasn't two people at opposite ends of the line. Instead, it was baby at one end and something like a magnet at the other, creating sounds for baby to do a small dance. So as baby danced, the screen displayed the show for Bisola, who kept saying that baby looked like he was whispering something all the time. When she was thirty-eight weeks gone and went once more to watch baby whispering away, she had pointed at the screen and laughed. "Hehehe, how the gossip has finally grown tired. Mama is here now. Talk."

Today the technician was quiet. He pushed the cob along the dark midline of Bisola's stomach. He paused, probed again. Bisola turned her eyes from the screen and worked out that baby may have forgotten his dance steps today. The technician left the room and returned with a nurse. The nurse made the technician move the cob up and down again, studying the screen all the while. She finally turned to Bisola and helped her sit up. Baby wasn't breathing, the woman said. There was no heartbeat.

But Bisola said it couldn't be. Only last night she had dreamed of baby, with a full head of hair like his father, small wet lips, and short slender fingers. She had dressed him in a jumper made from wax print and greased his hair with Vaseline mixed with palm kernel oil. He was colored a little like a grapefruit. He liked to be fed all the time and slept little. When he slept he made fists with his hands. Baby showed her these things because he wanted there to be an understanding between them before he made his appearance. He knew she knew little about babies, had learned nothing in the last forty-something years she'd been without a husband. Baby knew, baby knew. The cob machine was just something to make him dance when he pleased. And today, right where they sat across from this nosy screen, baby wanted a rest from sending last night's message.

The nurse led Bisola to see the doctor, who examined her on a gurney and finally wrote her a prescription. Still explaining that these things happened without warning, to women across all ages and ethnic groups, the nurse held Bisola's hand and led her down the blocks to the pharmacy. She told the story of her own niece, whose baby had been dead two weeks in her womb before the cob machine found out. Her niece had gone on to have three healthy children after that. So there was yet hope if Bisola took care of things early enough to start over. The pharmacist handed her a transparent pouch containing two small white tablets, each one six-sided with a thin vertical groove in the center. Bisola asked the nurse on their way out, "What's the medicine for, na?"

"It's to make your womb soft. Take them this evening and come back in two days like the doctor said."

In the zinc shed, before they packed up her batter pans for the day, Bisola told Osei what the hospital people had said about baby and his dancing. Osei took the pouch from her and said he was throwing away the medicine. Bisola agreed, surprised he could still read her mind this quickly despite the four years and eight months they'd been married. Perhaps that was what these younger men were good for, especially when one single-handedly set up their barbershops, bought them motorcycles, and kept them well fed and clothed.

First he read her mind about throwing away the medicine. Next he read her mind about getting a prayer ticket from the once-dead pastor who advertised on the radio. Hence, the next day, before she went to open up shop at the Power Joint, Osei rode her to the defunct factory site. He waited outside to get some fresh air as she received an initial analysis from the pastor, as well as a prayer schedule.

Two days down, one to go.

Bisola shuffled down the line of chairs in the anteroom, taking the yams and chicken as she went.

As she settled her hand yet again on her middle, she saw there was a commotion to her right—people arguing about a seat. It was Osei, speaking in placating tones to a burly man who was next in line after Bisola. He explained that Bisola was his wife and they were together. The man finally shrugged and Osei approached. Bisola saw the fresh sheen of his reapplied hair grease, the soft curve of his just-fed belly showing beneath his shirt. She felt panic that he had cut short his air-taking time just as she was close to entering the pastor's office. As he sat next to her, she gently nudged his side with her elbow and smiled tiredly.

He held the food flask in his lap, looking straight ahead. "Bisi, I ate the akara and gizzards."

She nodded. "You were hungry."

"Yes. But there's some left."

"We'll eat that when we get home."

"Yes, to celebrate."

They shifted down three more seats within forty minutes,

till Bisola was next in line and the enforcer waved her ahead. Bisola was conscious of Osei breathing heavily behind her as they entered the pastor's office, his shoes dragging in post-meal stupor. A woman materialized and shut the door after them. She had a face Biosla knew well: the pastor's attendant, dressed in a brown frock belted in the middle with a smooth black sash. A tall woman with a muscled visage, she seemed to have an established camaraderie with Bisola, to whom she spoke cordial words of welcome. She accepted the chicken and yams, saying, "The pastor will see you now."

The office itself was orange-lit from the drawn curtains and fat candles burning from the floor corners. In the middle stood the only furnishing: a sprawling altar the size of two standard desks laid side by side. It was decked in white cloth, with a leather-bound Bible and sixteen candles along the rim. A cubicle cordoned off with hospital-blue curtains was stationed on left side of the table, and it was from here that the pastor materialized. He swept aside the blue cloth with one hand, stepping into the orange light with short thudding strides. Immediately, Bisola took off her shoes and kneeled before him, hands upraised. "Pastor!"

"Daughter Bisola," the man said in a lazy, syrupy voice that seemed to make the candle flames hold still for an instant. He was a man of average height with strangely large hands. His eyes sat deep in his face so that when they roved in his head, he looked like a toy straining against tight screws. He drew closer, placed a hand on Bisola's head as he muttered a few words: "Glory, glory. Our God has conquered death."

Bisola cried out, "Save my baby, Pastor!"

"Your baby lives if God says so. I've already told you that, daughter Bisola. Get up."

Panting, Bisola stood.

The muscled attendant in the frock came forward. "Place the money on the altar," she said.

Bisola reached into the neckline of her dress and pulled out a wad of notes from where she'd tucked them into her brassiere. She deposited the rolls on the table, then started straightening the bills with shaking fingers.

Osei, who until now had been rooted to a spot not far from the door, hurried forward to help Bisola.

"Leave it." The pastor waved a hand and turned to the attendant. "Is the water ready?"

Between the altar and a fat candle in a corner was a large plastic tub, large enough to hold a squatting adult. A pail of water sat by the tub, and a small scoop floated on the surface like a miniature boat. As if she understood what was required of her, Bisola began to lift her dress over her head. Osei's lips flapped like a fish out of water. Without thinking, he took a step toward Bisola, but the pastor's voice stopped him.

"Ah, the husband. Isn't she doing this for the both of you?"

Bisola stood stiff in a half-slip and thick-strapped brassiere. The attendant led her by the hand as they circled the altar three times in long strides. After the third round, they were back to their earlier spot before the plastic tub. The pastor raised a song, "*Behold the resurrecting power of the Almighty,*" as Bisola stepped into the tub and kneeled. The attendant gently peeled off her half-slip and brassiere, and Osei watched as parts he thought were known only to him—Bisola's hulking breasts pinnacled with dark-brown areolas; her hairy thighs, gnarled as old forest trees; her stout buttocks, his volleyballs—all tumbled out of her underwear in the full gaze of the pastor and the woman in the brown frock.

The frocked woman was the one who doused Bisola with holy anointing oil before pouring the water from the pail over her. The pastor paused his singing. "Wait, let the husband do that," he said.

The woman walked over, handed the scoop to Osei, who now drew forward, no longer able to feel his legs. He tipped the scoop into the pail, poured water over his wife, and saw her shiver as if cold, despite the warmth of the room. As Osei poured, the pastor went to work. He laid his large hands on Bisola's head first, then her forehead, jaw, neck, and shoulders. Lower and lower he went, till her whole body was covered from front to back with the resurrecting essence of the third day. He commanded the earth to release the baby's trapped soul, and then commanded the mother's body to reabsorb the soul. Bisola belched and belched, all of the pent-up gas unfurling itself at the combined sensations of water and hands cascading down her body. At the end, she stepped out of the tub gleaming with oil that smelled like incense. The attendant helped her into her clothes, telling Bisola that she was strong, she had held on till the end, and she was now being rewarded. Before he disappeared behind the cubicle to ready himself for the next supplicant, the pastor gave Bisola a bottle of curry-smelling oil and told her to place it under her pillow before she went in for delivery the first day of the following week. The bottle was calibrated, and for every night she had it, the oil was meant to drop a notch. If she ever woke up to see the oil hadn't dropped, she was to phone her husband and hurry to the hospital before the sun rose high in the sky. The pastor's deep eyes glowed as he retreated behind the blue curtains.

Bisola turned to the attendant. "So will I feel baby kick now?"

"Of course!" The attendant took one of Bisola's hands and placed it over her stomach. Bisola waited for the familiar thud. She moved her hand all over, thinking the restarted heart may have shifted with the force of all that spiritual activity. She waited some more. "Osei, come and feel . . ."

But Osei was already beside her, feeling too for the thud. Suddenly he said, "Yes! Yes!"

"What?" Bisola stared at him. "You feel it then?"

"Thank you. Oh, thank you!" Osei was now at the door, where he had left the half-empty food flask on the floor. He grabbed it and pushed it at the attendant. "Thank you for helping us." Then he was out of the office in a flash.

The attendant was laughing. "All this for me?" she asked, holding onto the flask with both arms.

Bisola called out to Osei. She hurried after him, past the anteroom where the crowd calmly shifted in their chairs, past the corridor with framed words of hope, and past the thick sweat of clamoring desperation in the reception lobby. Outside, she didn't try to talk to him until they got to where he had parked the motorcycle. He had chained it to a massive, useless chunk of metal that once belonged in the factory. As Osei unlocked the chain and rolled out the motorcycle, Bisola saw that he had his face turned into his shirt collar. He was sobbing. But he still gripped the handlebars like he was waiting for her to embark. Bisola didn't come close. The silence of the late night, except for the sounds of the ruckus from the lobby a distance away, bubbled in the rift between them. Finally she said, "It's all for a miracle. And miracles cost more, my husband. What would you have me do?"

"Bisi. Oh, Bisi," Osei mumbled.

Bisola approached, climbed onto the back seat, and anchored the cycle with her weight so he could get on with ease. It was then she noticed that the smell filling her nose was not his oranges or hair grease, but the lingering fragrance of incense from the tub.

"But it's also like a hospital, not so? I'm their open farm and can't run from the cutlasses and knives." She shifted her weight on the motorcycle, placed a hand on the last spot the attendant had positioned it on her stomach. "We will go home now, wait for the oil to drop in the morning. And we must never, ever be late, my husband. The oil will drop. You'll see."

EDEN

BY UCHE OKONKWO

Obalende

Madu had never reached into the back of the videocassette cupboard: that dark, dusty place where the films were older than God. But today, bored and desperate not to rewatch another film—*Nneka the Pretty Serpent*, *Terminator 2*, *Mortal Kombat*—with his sister Ifechi, he got on his knees in front of the cupboard and thrust his hand in, taking out the first tape he touched. The cassette had his father's initials on its side, written in black ink on a strip of adhesive paper.

Ifechi peered at it. "What film is that?"

Holding the cassette up to his face, Madu read the title: *A Taste of Paradise*.

Ifechi hesitated. "Madu . . ." she warned, "it's Daddy's film."

"So what?"

Madu stood and took the tape out of its case, noticing, through the clear plastic in the cassette's center, that both spools had almost an equal amount of tape around them. He slipped the tape into the player and pressed play.

"Won't you rewind it?" Ifechi asked.

"Let's see what kind of film it is first."

They waited as the familiar whirring sound started from the cassette player. Then a massive penis filled the screen.

"Jesus!" Madu shrieked, jumping back and away from

the TV without taking his eyes off it. His sister stood frozen, watching the screen like it would rip her into a million pieces if she dared to turn away. For a while, the only sounds in the living room were the hum of the cassette player and the creaking of the ceiling fan as the blades turned. The old TV was acting up again—there was no sound. Madu crept toward the set and brought his palm down against its side twice, sharply, like he'd seen their father do many times to get the speakers to function. It worked. They heard moaning sounds carried on waves of fluty background music.

Two white men, one white woman, a white bed, white walls, a white floor littered with long-stemmed red roses, all the more stark against so much white. The woman lay writhing on the bed, her legs spread wide as she touched herself. Ifechi, distressed to find that the exposed flesh between the woman's legs was the same pink as her best pinafore, decided that yellow was her new favorite color. One of the men straddled the woman's head and she took his penis in her mouth.

"She's licking it, sha!" Madu cried, his mouth hanging open.

The second man, who'd stood leaning against a wall watching the other two while he stroked his penis, bent to pick up a rose. He held it in one hand, and with the thumb and forefinger of the other he stroked the rose's unnaturally smooth stem: up, down, then up and down again. He kneeled between the woman's legs and took the hand he found there, sucking on each finger like she'd dipped them in chocolate. Then he trailed the flower up the woman's thigh.

"Hei!" Ifechi said as the rose stem disappeared beneath the patch of blond pubic hair between the woman's legs. "Is it not paining her?"

"It's not paining her," Madu replied without looking at his sister. "She would have told them to stop."

"Madu," Ifechi said, with a nervous glance at the door, "what if Aunty Hope comes?"

Aunty Hope ran the small hair salon downstairs, and she looked in on the children while their parents were at work. It was also her job to make sure that the children did not mix with the urchins, as their father liked to call the happy, unkempt bunch that ran about the neighborhood most afternoons, rolling tires down the streets.

With the children on holiday, Aunty Hope had to check on them more often. Some days she would march them down to her salon and have them sit there for hours with their books. Aunty Hope's moods were tied to the frequent and unannounced NEPA power cuts: happy when there was power, surly otherwise. Like many of the residents and small businesses in their Obalende neighborhood, Aunty Hope could not afford a generator.

Sometimes Aunty Hope would invite the children to watch her work. Ifechi liked watching her comb creamy white relaxer into the women's hair and felt a malicious delight when they scrunched up their faces as it started to burn. At seven, Ifechi was not allowed to have her hair relaxed. She longed to turn ten, like Madu. She would be a big girl then.

"Go and lock the door," Madu said now, his eyes still on the TV. Ifechi stayed put, frowning and shifting her weight from one foot to the other. Madu spun around to face her. "Ifechi, go and lock the door, and stop acting stupid!"

Ifechi stomped to the front door, locked it, and returned to her place, her brother's glare following her.

"Idiot," he muttered, before turning to the TV again.

Ifechi was finding it hard to breathe. The room seemed to get warmer, the air thicker, as the minutes passed. The woman on the screen was on her hands and knees now, one man behind her, the other in front. "I don't want to watch anymore," Ifechi said, her voice hoarse with unshed tears.

"Then stop watching," Madu said. "Silly baby."

Ifechi did not turn away.

Uncle Zubby and Aunty Agodi lived in a big white house on Glover Road in Ikoyi. Even though it was only a few minutes from their home in Obalende, Madu and Ifechi's parents were careful not to take the family visiting too often. "Before they think we only visit for their light and AC," their mother would say, with an edge to her voice.

Madu and Ifechi enjoyed visiting Uncle Zubby and Aunty Agodi. They would pile into their father's Santana and ride with the windows down—the car's AC had been broken for as long as the children could remember—inhaling the breeze and exhaust smoke blowing in their faces. They would look out the window as they passed the police barracks and the market on their muddy street, the sights and smells at once teasing and assaulting. On Ikoyi Road, they would pass the immigration office, quiet and deserted on the weekend, and then the massive building of the old Federal Secretariat compound, with almond trees lining the fence and dotting the grounds. It was around this point that the noise and grime of Obalende began to give way to Ikoyi's genteel influence. The streets grew quieter, with actual sidewalks and streetlights that mostly worked. Colonial-style houses stood proud in vast tree-lined compounds with green lawns. Even the air felt different. The children would often spot white people in shorts and canvas shoes walking exotic-looking dogs, and they would stare at the dog-walkers until they became flecks of white in the distance. Madu liked to imagine that the oyinbos were never able to go beyond the secretariat. That if they tried, some unseen, all-powerful barrier would literally stop them, and they would turn around and walk their dogs back to Ikoyi.

Madu adored Uncle Zubby and Aunty Agodi's big home, with the big generator that had its own house. He didn't mind that the couple had no children for him and Ifechi to play with, even though his mother often said how unfortunate this was. For Madu, it was enough that they always had electricity in their house. Plus, his uncle had loads of video games, and comic books that he let Madu borrow and not return.

Ifechi liked Uncle Zubby. She liked Aunty Agodi too—she made the best chin-chin in the world!—but she liked her uncle more. He reminded her of Father Christmas, with his lips buried beneath a forest of graying beard. Every time the beard parted to let him speak, Ifechi would feign surprise to find his lips there. Uncle Zubby always greeted her with a hug, and Ifechi would raise her forehead and rub her skin against the crisp hairs on his chin.

As they often did on these visits, the adults left Madu and Ifechi in the smaller living room with soft drinks, a platter of chin-chin, and the TV, while they sat and talked in the larger one. Today Ifechi sat sipping her Fanta, wishing her brother would settle on a channel; he'd been fiddling with the TV remote since they got there. She listened to the voices of the adults drifting in from the next room, and she remembered the conversation she had overheard last week.

"Madu."

"What?"

"Come, let me tell you something." Ifechi glanced at the doorway to make sure nobody was coming.

"You come here," Madu said as he changed channels again. Ifechi sighed and shuffled closer to her brother on the couch.

"Do you know," Ifechi started, her voice low, "that when a girl becomes a big girl, if a boy touches her she will get pregnant?"

Madu stared at Ifechi in reproving silence.

"Just touch like this-o," Ifechi said, poking her brother's thigh to demonstrate.

"You're stupid."

"But it's true! I heard Mummy and Clementina's mummy saying it. Remember that day that Mummy said we should read our science books after church; that day the rain fell? When I went to the kitchen to drink water, I heard them. They didn't see me, but I heard them."

Madu found a channel showing *Mighty Morphin Power Rangers*. He placed the remote beside him on the couch. "So, you're an eavesdropper," he said.

"What's *eavesdropper*?"

"Olodo, don't they teach you English in primary three?"

"You're abusing me, abi? Okay, I won't tell you anything again." Ifechi sat back with a pout, her hands folded across her chest.

"Okay, sorry," Madu said. "Sorry. Tell me."

Ifechi's eyes went bright as she turned to her brother again. "They were saying that one of their friend's daughters got pregnant without a father. They said that all the boys in Lagos have touched her, that's why they don't now know which one is the father."

"Oh, so you mean if I touch you now you will get pregnant?" Madu laughed as he pressed his sister's neck. "I've touched you; now you're pregnant."

"No jor!" Ifechi said, frowning at her brother's show of ignorance. "They said it's when somebody is a big girl. I'm not a big girl yet."

"And how will you know when you become a big girl?"

Ifechi glanced at the door again. "You did not hear what Clementina's mummy said. She said that Clementina . . . that blood was coming out of Clementina's pee-pee. That means she is now a big girl. If you see her in school when we resume, better don't touch her."

"Why are you lying, Ifechi? How can a person pee blood?"

"Shhhh! I'm not lying, that's what they said. Clementina's mummy said she told Clementina that if a boy touches her she will become pregnant. And Mummy said she will tell me the same thing too when I'm a big girl."

"So where does the blood come from? Will there be a wound inside your tummy?"

"Me, I don't know, but that's what they said."

Madu contemplated this for a moment. "So after you start peeing blood, if I touch you, you will get pregnant?"

Ifechi blinked up at the ceiling and considered the question. "No," she decided. "Because you're my brother. If it's another boy, then I will get pregnant. Then my tummy will swell like a watermelon and my pee-pee will tear when the baby is coming out."

"Ifechi!"

"But that's what they said—it's not me that said it!"

Madu rolled his eyes and turned back to the TV. But he was curious and so, even though he hadn't decided if he believed his sister, he asked, "But . . . what if a boy touches you by mistake? Just by mistake-o."

"I will still get pregnant," Ifechi responded with quiet certainty, her lips turned down at the corners. "That means that once I become a big girl I won't allow any boy to come near me. And you too, don't be touching girls anyhow." She pulled her earlobe for emphasis. "Because you can't know who is big."

Madu bit his lower lip. "How do I know you're even telling the truth?"

Ifechi shrugged. "I've told you. If you like, don't hear. Mummy said that if any of her children disgrace her she will send us back to our father in heaven."

They watched the TV in silence for a few minutes.

"Madu?"

"What?"

"Will Mummy send us to heaven if they catch us watching those bad films?"

Madu reached for a handful of chin-chin and stuffed it in his mouth.

One rainy night when there was no electricity, the children played Catch the Light with their father. Their mother lay on the couch, laughing and shouting warnings—"Careful, watch her head!" Catch the Light was their game, invented by their father for nights like this, when the electricity was gone and there was a sense of camaraderie. He would put out the candles and let the warm darkness surround them. Then he would turn on his flashlight and move the beam all around the room, the children scrambling to touch it with their hands or feet. It was the only game they played together.

The stakes were high on this night. Their father had promised the winner three over-the-head spins, to be redeemed at any time of the winner's choosing. Madu and Ifechi loved being held above the head of their tall father and spun, loved opening their eyes to see the furniture, barely discernible in the dark, whirling around them. They loved the dizzying sensation that remained after they were set down gently, like honey lingering on their tongues. But most of all they loved the chafing feel of their father's palms as he gripped them, and they imagined that his hands left an imprint on them that remained long after he let go.

The children rushed from spot to spot, shrieking and stretching their limbs toward the light. But just when they thought they'd got it, the light would move away and they would laugh out their frustration. The light was all they could see, and they followed wherever it went, sometimes bumping into each other and their father.

At one point their father directed the beam of light to a spot close to his feet. As the children rushed forward, Ifechi in front, Madu bumped into her, sending her face into the region of their father's crotch.

Ifechi felt her cheek make contact with her father's penis through his shorts, and she straightened up at once. She stifled the urge to run, to cover the offending cheek with her palm. She glanced at her mother's dark form on the couch; it was still. Had she seen? Ifechi tried to find her father's face in the gloom, certain that he knew. But he was still moving the light, and Madu was still running and screaming.

When their father was ready to let someone win, he chose Madu. Their father picked him up and spun him over his head, both of them laughing while Ifechi watched with remorse from her place on the ground.

When the dreams first started—dreams of thick pubic hairs in many colors, and breasts with dusky, hard-looking peaks that he imagined would taste like cola candy—Madu had considered telling Ifechi about them. But how would she help? All she knew how to do was cry. Madu did not consider telling his parents: his father would send for his whip, and his mother would make him kneel with his hands raised for hours, and then command him to fill a twenty-page notebook with the words, *I WILL NOT BE A BAD BOY.*

In this latest dream, a woman looked up from the penis she'd been painting with her tongue, turned in his direction, and stared into his eyes. She smiled and beckoned with an index finger. Madu woke up to find his heart pounding and his penis straining against his pajama bottoms. He glanced at Ifechi's bed across from his and, satisfied that she was asleep, felt the unfamiliar hardness with a tentative hand, awe and dread churning inside him. When Madu noticed that it felt good touching himself, he shoved his hands under his pillow, squeezing his eyes shut as he murmured Hail Marys. After twenty slow recitals Madu's penis went back to normal.

He let out a sigh and slept like an innocent.

Madu and Ifechi were watching *Pussy Palace* that afternoon—with their parents at work, the front door locked, and Aunty Hope busy in her salon—when the TV screen went dead. Like people emerging from a cave into daylight, the children looked up at the ceiling fan that was slowing to a stop above their heads. They were thinking the same thing.

"Don't worry," Madu said, as much for his own comfort as for his sister's. "NEPA will bring back the light before Mummy and Daddy come back . . . Don't worry."

The hours passed and the electricity did not return. The tape player stayed silent and stoic as Madu examined it with angry eyes, pushing the eject button over and over, lifting the player up from its stand, turning it upside down, rubbing the top of it, as though to coax it into spitting out the cassette.

"Hei, God . . ." Ifechi prayed-sang every few minutes, trying not to cry because she knew it would annoy Madu, "please let NEPA bring back the light before Mummy and Daddy come."

But by six thirty when their parents returned, all the praying and glaring had neither caused the electricity to return nor the cassette to eject itself from the machine.

All evening, Madu and Ifechi tiptoed around their mother while she made dinner. They offered their help with sweet smiles and worried her with questions, which she answered with a slightly tortured air. When she'd had enough she waved them out of the kitchen with a stew-covered ladle.

As the family sat down to eat, Madu and Ifechi exchanged nervous glances. When their father cleared his throat to say grace, they lowered their eyelids but kept their eyes open, watching the candlelight play on their parents' faces.

The children picked at their dinner of boiled yams and tomato stew with much ceremony, making their cutlery clink busily against the ceramic plates. But their mother wasn't fooled.

"Why aren't you two eating?" she asked.

"We're full, Mummy," Ifechi said.

"Full? When you've not even eaten anything?" Their mother frowned as she reached forward and felt their necks with the back of her hand, Madu's first, then Ifechi's. "Are you not feeling well?"

"We're well, Mummy," they chorused. Not feeling well meant visits to the hospital and injections. They shoveled down their food.

Before their mother could make more of a fuss, the ceiling fan started to turn, sending the flames of the candles into a mad dance. The house hummed with the sound of working appliances. The children sat very still while their mother stood, with a grateful sigh, to close the drapes and turn on the lights.

"My friend, blow out the candles," their father scolded

Madu. "Or is your mouth too heavy you're waiting for the fan to do it?"

After dinner, their father settled down in front of the TV for the evening news while their mother did the dishes. Madu and Ifechi stayed up in the living room with their father long after their mother had gone to bed, watching over the tape player and the evidence inside it, pretending to be taken with the documentary that was showing. It was only a matter of time; their father would get up to go to the toilet, or to get something out of his room.

After the documentary, their father looked at Madu and Ifechi, as though noticing their presence for the first time since dinner.

"It's almost ten," he said. "You two go to bed."

"Daddy, please, we're not feeling sleepy yet," Ifechi begged.

"And we're still on holiday," Madu added.

"Did you hear what I just said?" Their father leaned forward in his chair. The children got up and shuffled out of the living room, then hid in the doorway peeping at him. Without taking his eyes off the TV, he called out, "Madu, Ifechi—if I come out and find you still standing there, ehn . . ."

The children ran into their room and lay down in silence, listening for sounds from the living room. They thought they heard their father moving about and hoped he was going to bed. But they didn't hear any doors open or shut.

"What if Daddy . . ." Ifechi whispered.

"Shhh!"

Apart from the thumping in their chests the children could hear nothing. They lay quiet for what felt like a very long time. Soon, Ifechi began to drift off to sleep. But the next sound wiped every trace of sleep from her eyes and almost stopped her brother's heart.

"Madu! Ifechi!"

Ifechi felt hot liquid seep between her legs and she clamped her thighs together. "Madu! Daddy is calling us," she whined.

"Shut up," Madu hissed. "Act as if you're sleeping."

"Madu! Ifechi! Come out here now!" Their father's voice was closer; they could hear his footsteps approaching their door.

"Madu," Ifechi pleaded.

"Shut up and close your eyes," Madu said. "Don't say anything."

The children's bedroom door flew open, ricocheted against the wall. Their father filled the doorway.

"Both of you, get up right now!"

Madu blinked up at his father's face. "Yes, Daddy?" he said, attempting a sleepy murmur. Ifechi, with her wide eyes and trembling lips, was less convincing.

"Get out now! To the parlor!" their father barked.

They stumbled out of their beds as their mother came to the door. "Chuma," she said to their father, "what is it?"

He gave no reply. He followed behind Madu and Ifechi as they shuffled into the living room. Their mother joined them seconds later.

"Who has been watching this film?" their father asked, brandishing the cassette tape.

Ifechi glanced up from her feet to her brother's face. Maybe if she confessed quickly their father would have mercy. She could tell the truth and shame the devil. She could say it was Madu's idea, which was the truth. But if she did that Madu would never talk to her again.

"What film is that? Let me see," their mother said. She stepped closer and took the tape from their father. She read the title, and her body grew tense. She gave her husband a long, pointed glare as she held out the cassette to him. He took it, but only when he looked away did their mother turn to Madu and Ifechi.

"So I have been breeding dirty maggots in this house, ehn?" she said. "Instead of reading your books, this is what you spend your time doing when we are at work?"

"This is the last time I will ask both of you," their father said. "Who watched this film?"

Ifechi looked at the tape in her father's hand. His palm now covered the portion of paper on the cassette that had his initials.

"It was me."

Ifechi gasped and snapped her head up to look at her brother. He was staring into the space in front of him.

"Only you, Madu?" their father asked after a brief silence. He turned to Ifechi. "What about you?"

"She was with Aunty Hope," Madu answered for his sister.

"Is it true?" their mother asked Ifechi, who could only nod. She knew her voice would fail her if she tried to speak.

"Ifechi, go to my room and bring my koboko," their father commanded.

Ifechi managed to steady her legs and direct them out of the living room. She'd always loved the smell of her parents' bedroom—camphor and a blend of their perfumes. But as she entered their room this time she took quick, shallow breaths. She reached into the floor of her father's wardrobe for the whip: Mr. Koboko, as they called it when they were being playful. But there was nothing playful about the rough brown leather of the whip when it stung the skin, the three strands, like tentacles, curling around limbs and leaving welts wherever they touched. Ifechi felt lightheaded at the thought of the koboko hitting her brother's flesh. She stumbled in the bedroom doorway on her way out and paused to gather herself. Still, her hands shook as she presented the whip to her father, careful not to make contact with his skin.

"Now go to your room," he said to her.

"No," their mother snapped. "Let her watch so she can learn."

So Ifechi watched as her brother lowered his pajama bottoms and placed his palms against the nearest wall. Their father raised his hand with the koboko in it, and as he let it come down on Madu's buttocks Ifechi squeezed her eyes shut. She couldn't see, but she could hear—the whoosh of the whip, her father's grunts, her brother's gasps. After six lashes Madu started to cry. Tears stung Ifechi's eyes and she squeezed them even tighter, but the tears found a way to seep through. By the tenth stroke Madu was begging, his voice choked with phlegm: "Please, Daddy! Daddy, please, please, I won't do it again!"

Their father's response was a warning: "If you rub your buttocks, I will start counting from one." That was when Ifechi stopped counting.

When it was finally over Ifechi felt like her legs would crumple beneath her. Their mother's was the only dry face in the room; their father's was dripping with sweat. He let the koboko fall from his hand, like he'd purged himself of something.

"What do you say?" their mother asked.

Ifechi looked from her to Madu as the seconds stretched into an eternity.

"What do you say?" she asked again, her tone sharp this time.

Madu stared at the ground. When he opened his mouth his words were almost inaudible. "Thank you, Mummy. Thank you, Daddy."

They were sent to their room. With each shaky step Madu took he grew bigger in Ifechi's eyes—her big, strong brother who would protect her from the world. She promised to never annoy him ever again, swore she would do anything for him.

Madu flopped onto his bed, burying his face in his arms. Ifechi could hear his sobs, hear the sound of their parents trying to argue quietly in the living room. She sat on the floor beside Madu's bed, rubbing his head and chanting, "Madu, sorry. Madu, sorry . . ." Seeing that her brother was not comforted, Ifechi went to their dressing table and grabbed the tub of Vaseline, because Vaseline could heal anything.

"Madu, should I rub Vaseline on your bum-bum?"

Ifechi got no response. When she started to tug on Madu's pajama bottoms, his arm shot out of nowhere, knocking the tub of Vaseline out of her hand and across the room where it crashed into the wall.

It was two weeks later and school had reopened after the long holidays. Madu and Ifechi's school was on a side street off St. Gregory's College Road. Even though Obalende Primary School was much closer to their home, their parents would not hear of it. "I can't have my children mixing with those urchins," their father had said once to a neighbor who'd expressed concern at the distance Madu and Ifechi had to walk every school day. Before their mother got a job she used to be around to take them to and from school. Now she only dropped them off in the mornings, with prayers and admonitions to guide them on their way back home: *Don't talk to strangers, look properly before crossing, never pick any money or strange object from the ground, never* ever *ride on an okada to get home.*

The first few times they'd walked back home on their own

Madu had murmured his mother's warnings like a mantra, all the way from St. Gregory's College Road, to Obalende Roundabout, to Forest Street, and onto Ijeh Village Road. Gripping his sister's hand he'd weave through throngs of people at the bus stops. He'd attach himself, his sister in tow, to unwitting adults and cross the busy roads with them.

But those days felt like a long time ago to Madu. Removed now from the shelter of his parents' cars, he had grown accustomed to the pulsating mass that was Obalende, with its countless yellow danfos and molues, conductors courting passengers to faraway destinations across the city—Oshodi, Ikeja, Yaba—traders wooing passersby with wares that could cure anything.

Madu and Ifechi walked back home from school in the afternoon heat. As they did most days, they walked in silence until they got onto their street, where Madu let go of Ifechi's hand and slowed their pace.

Ifechi hopped onto the rim of the gutter that ran beside the road and walked on it. She spread her arms for balance as she looked down into the gutter, at the litter and grime inside it. After a while, Madu pulled his sister off the rim and close to his side. "There's this girl in my class," he said. "She showed me her panties today, during break."

"Haa!" Ifechi gasped, covering her mouth with the palm of one hand. She stopped walking, forcing Madu to stop too. "Why? What were you doing?"

Madu shrugged. "Nothing. We were just playing. I asked her what color they were, and she raised up her uniform and showed me." Madu eyed his sister. "What? Why are you saying *haa* like that?"

"Madu . . . have you forgotten what happened with Daddy's films?"

"So what? This wasn't a film."

"But it's still bad! Did you touch her?" Madu resumed walking, and Ifechi went on as she followed. "Madu, Mummy said I should tell her if you do anything bad again-o."

Madu spun to face his sister, and she noticed for the first time how much like their father he looked. She took a small step back.

"Good girl," Madu sneered. "So you want to report me to Mummy now, because I covered for you. Didn't we watch those films together? And wasn't it me and you that went back to look for *Pussy Palace* even after Daddy beat me? You would have still continued to watch with me if Daddy didn't remove the films from the cupboard. But you are now the good one, and Madu is bad."

"No," Ifechi muttered, staring at her feet.

"You're just a baby. So you can run and tell Mummy if you want. That's what a baby would do." Madu leaned toward his sister, bringing his face as close to hers as possible without their skins touching. "*Baaaabyyyy.*"

He stalked off and Ifechi stood watching him, tears filling her eyes. She blinked them away and ran after him.

They were in bed that night when Madu heard their bedroom door open. He propped himself up on his elbows just in time to see Ifechi slip out the door. The sound of the TV floated in from the living room. And then all went quiet.

Several minutes passed before Madu got out of bed to follow after her. But then he heard the lash of the koboko, and Ifechi's cry right after. He froze as it slowly dawned on him what Ifechi must have done. It was foolish. *She* was foolish. Still, Madu couldn't help feeling a grudging admiration for his foolish little sister.

He was sitting up on his bed when Ifechi returned. He could only see a silhouette of her in the darkened room but he knew her legs would feel like melting wax, pain pulsing through every nerve. He knew that the heat would spread from her behind, infecting the rest of her like a fever.

She fell facedown onto her bed, crying, her legs hanging out over the frame. Madu stood and went to the dresser. He felt around the top of it until his fingers touched the tub of Vaseline. He picked it up and took off the lid. Then he went to Ifechi and raised the hem of her nightie. She shoved it back down and shifted an inch or two on her bed, away from Madu. He waited a few seconds before trying again, and this time Ifechi let him raise her nightie until it was halfway up her back. He scooped up some Vaseline with his right forefinger.

Ifechi flinched as Madu touched her skin. He paused for a moment, and then he began rubbing gently, his fingers making a steady circular motion on the mound of his sister's buttock. He found it mesmerizing, and not altogether unpleasant, the feel of skin against skin, the contact made even smoother by the Vaseline.

"Why did you tell them?" he asked.

He was on the second buttock when she answered. "Because I am bad too."

Madu's fingers went still as he contemplated his sister's words, the sureness with which she had said them. For the first time he could remember, he did not know how to feel.

He went back to rubbing, his fingers going around and around in an endless loop.

JOY

BY WALE LAWAL

Surulere

Near the end, you'd remember you forgave Joy—nothing too vivid, at best the memory would occur to you as fleeting as a hint. You'd recall the evening of her first transgression and that she believed you had forgotten about her being half-naked in your bedroom, trying on your clothes. And you'd despise yourself for this. You'd wish you had not stayed quiet, had not walked over to your side of the bedroom and picked up your phone from the dresser, when you should have slapped the girl across the room. Your mother always said you had a heart like an akara—you could go through fire and remain soft. Turns out your mother was right.

You didn't even know the girl's real name. But you knew it was Mama Lateef's style to give her girls English names once they arrived in Lagos. Mama Lateef, who supplied your mother with house girls when you were growing up, had once explained to your mother that English names made her clients comfortable; the least of her reasons being that names from the West bore neither secrets nor ancestral curses. In her line of business, English names were rivers old and without current; they couldn't possibly carry the dead.

Mama Lateef was in her sixties now and sat in your living room repeating the same things she had told your mother all those years ago, and then she suggested that you and your husband could call the girl Joy.

"Joy?" you said, and the girl nodded on impulse.

"Ṣ'o ri?" Mama Lateef said, amused. "The girl has already taken the name."

Joy was from Cotonou, in Benin. As far as you knew, she had no family, as was typical of Mama Lateef's girls. She was slim, not pretty, with big marble eyes and even bigger pink lips. She spoke Fon, Yoruba, and some French, and her English, which was barely basic, Mama Lateef swore would improve quickly. According to Mama Lateef, Joy was nineteen, though you sensed the girl was younger: fourteen, sixteen at the most. Her age troubled you, and you told Mama Lateef that you needed to discuss this with your husband first; and, thinking you were going to ask for his permission, Mama Lateef said she understood.

But Joy was disappointed, would sulk as if the entire world had collapsed on her tiny frame. And in a moment of weakness at the end of your meeting, you assured Joy that you liked her. That your delaying was for her own good. Later in the evening, Yinka, your husband, suggested that you take the girl anyway. What did it matter if she was underage? Aimọye eyan: her type see much worse in Lagos than a young couple, and surely it wouldn't be helpful to leave her with Mama Lateef, who had all kinds of clients.

"She's better off living with people like us," he said. "We'll feed her well, can even send her to school. After all, we only really need her to help around for when the baby comes."

He was *that* good, quick-thinking, quick with you; his buddies from university hadn't called him Papapa for no reason. The baby was your pressure point and the prospect of raising a child together always made the two of you happy. So that was how you settled the argument that night—happy.

That same night, you called Mama Lateef and told her you were interested in the girl, and the next day you hired her. Joy arrived in the morning, shortly after Yinka left for work, with two black polyethylene bags filled with her belongings, all of which she showed you—as was customary—with Mama Lateef as witness. Joy didn't come with much: three T-shirts, two skirts, a new toothbrush, a pair of green rubber slippers, a pair of black, worn-out leather flats, a Bible, an unopened pack of Always, and two pairs of underwear—no bras. Days later, Mama Lateef's reaction would still be fresh in your mind. "Bra nkọ? Bra da? Ṣe ere lo ro p'owa ṣe nibi ni? What nonsense!"

"She's a hardworking girl," Mama Lateef later said. "Ọmọ to da ni. You'll see, everybody lo ma n like ẹ." And before she left, Joy rose from where she had been kneeling, repacking her things, and embraced Mama Lateef. "Face your work, ṣ'o gbọ?" Mama Lateef said, holding her by her shoulders. She turned to you, smiling: "Sometimes, ẹ mọ, these girls forget."

Mama Lateef didn't exaggerate—Joy was extremely likable. Were she still alive, ọmọ to fa iṣe mọ'ra, your mother would have called her. She reminded you of Mercy, the girl who served your mother for years. A girl so loyal that when your mother tried to poison her husband, the girl swallowed both accusation and punishment without regret. And you hoped to make such a girl out of Joy. Once she got past her shyness, Joy aimed to please. She kneeled when she spoke and buried her eyes when she was spoken to. She smiled when you complimented her, and had a way of laughing into herself whenever she became the object of attention. She reminded you of a mimosa; quiet, delicate, she moved like a secret.

Yinka thought Joy was awesome (all men have a go-to adjective and that was his) and sharp. Her maths, he used to say, was on point. It was strangely entertaining the effect adding currency to random numbers had on her mental acuity; how, for Joy, the difference between genius and stupidity was the naira. She couldn't tell you twenty times five, but ask Joy N1,520 times fifteen and it was like NEPA had brought light behind her eyes—from her mouth, the girl churned numbers. So when you brought it up that Joy should attend a primary school in the area, Yinka agreed. More so, he offered to fund it.

The women in your book club liked Joy too. They made no comments about her and that was enough. The club met on the last Wednesday of every month, late in the afternoon, and rotated living rooms as venues. By the time they met Joy, it was your third meeting, and all five members including you were discussing *The Bluest Eye*. You hated it—not the book, which you had suggested at the previous meeting, but the book club. You had only joined because Yinka thought it would be good for you to be around other women. Plus, reading with them, he swore, would be a bonus since you had always wanted to get back into what used to be your favorite pastime. He thought, also, that the book club would get you some friends, the two of you being new in the neighborhood, and you being at home most of the time. But Yinka didn't know these women like you did, much less like you had come to know them after having read with them.

He didn't know how Bola, forty-two with Eucharia Anunobi eyebrows, openly gushed about Yinka's photographs and would always steer the conversation toward his role in your sex life. Yinka couldn't imagine a woman like

Nneka, thirty-eight, who treated her house help like garbage, and once, when the club met at her house, she asked the girl to kneel down and fly her arms *(for making me repeat myself,* Nneka had explained). And women like Ibukun and Jumoke, both your age, thirty-six, sickened you for how often they spoke about their pastor, *Daddy this* and *Daddy that.* But Yinka couldn't know that; after all, both women reminded you of his mother, whose company you enjoyed, as far as he was concerned. These women knew nothing about books. They were, after all, the kind who concluded that Toni Morrison had *tried* with *The Bluest Eye* (though Bola thought the punctuation could have been better), and meant it as a compliment.

It was September and the women were seated in your living room that Wednesday when it occurred to them that the next book should be *Joys of Motherhood* by Buchi Emecheta. Bola, who suggested it, claimed the idea just popped into her head. Moments later, Joy walked in with a tray of iced tea and Bola squealed that it must be more than coincidence: Joy. *Joys of . . .* If you rolled your eyes any farther back, they'd have thought you were Liz Benson in *Diamond Ring*. None of the other women had read *Joys of Motherhood* but Bola claimed her oldest daughter, who was in secondary school, had brought it home once.

"I haven't read it yet but it's a good book, well-written," she said. "Not like that last book—who even suggested it? Nneka, I'm sure it was you."

Nneka responded, "What do you mean by that?"

And Bola: "Nothing-o, don't mind me."

Nneka: "Before, nko? You see, it wasn't even me. But I don't blame you, we kuku know your memory is one-kind."

Everybody knew what Nneka meant. One way or another, Nneka, a classic eke, had gotten around to telling everyone in the book club how she suspected that Bola's husband wasn't the one responsible for Bola's children—everyone except Bola.

"Women, please!" cried Ibukun.

"We didn't come here to fight!" Jumoke added.

You left the women in the living room for your bedroom, where you had sent Joy to fetch your phone—the girl was taking too long.

The truth was, since you moved to Surulere you had been beset with melancholy. Sure, living there had its advantages, including the area's organic electricity, which compensated for the absence of actual electricity. For you especially, Surulere provided a unique proximity to Nigerian films and to your favorite actors and actresses, whom you ran into randomly at restaurants, salons, and supermarkets. Once, at a supermarket, a man you swore was Fred Amata had asked if you would like to star in a film he was producing, but you declined. Still, living in Surulere was nothing like living in Ikoyi had been, and Yinka would often remind you that deciding to sell the house in Dolphin Estate was the third-best decision the two of you had ever made, the first being to get married and the second being to have a child together. The book club only made things worse but, really, you preferred when the women fought to when they discussed books. The former was something they were actually good at.

You found yourself just as drawn to as you were repulsed by Jumoke. Jumoke, who described herself as pregnant-pregnant (because she had been pregnant for more than six months), and had mentioned to you that by the next meeting she would have delivered her fourth child. "How many months is it now?" she had once asked you, and you had replied that you would be three months pregnant in a week. Then she asked why you looked so tired already when you had two more trimesters to complete. She went on to tell you to eat more vegetables, fresh vegetables-o, and it didn't matter that you hadn't asked. The novelty of being pregnant—the effusive attention from onlookers, the platitudes, how you had become the American Embassy for unsolicited advice, the nausea—set you apart from the other women, far enough to recognize how so quickly you had become a Nollywood wife.

But there was Joy, who took your mind away from these things. Joy, who at night rubbed your feet with Chinese balm and in the mornings massaged your joints with hot, moist towels; Joy, whose fingers were nimble and deft; who, even as you swelled, looked at your naked body through a combination of zeal, envy, and adoration, your skin the color of salmon and hers, peat. Joy, who took to learning the mechanics of your body with steadfastness, and lotioned your back as though the skin around it was of silk tapestry and hers to keep. And you wondered: *Would she do anything for me? Could she be my own Mercy?*

The same Joy, you had observed, was growing into a remarkable girl. She had gained some weight, some light around her cheeks, plump to her breasts, and wore confidence like an ipele of emeralds around her shoulders. It would make you laugh if it didn't terrify you a little. They were always girls, never women, your mother had cautioned you—about the Joys of the world. There can only be one woman in any household, even your father with his four wives ensured each had hers. "So jẹ ki o ye ẹ dada," she always told you. "Such girls don't need your pity or friendship." And how—for she had told you this when you were at that age where daughters believe themselves to be the Euodia to their mothers' Syntyche and challenge them—you pitied and befriended those girls still.

But Joy was childlike, you'd tell yourself. Nothing like the girls your mother had employed, you reminded yourself as you walked to your bedroom that evening. She was almost like a younger sister, you thought, before wondering how difficult it could be to find a phone you had left on the dresser. You needed to call Yinka, to ask him what he'd like to eat when he got home, and you were already behind schedule, five p.m. instead of four.

"Sorry, ma, sorry, ma," you started hearing as soon as you entered the room, and that was when you saw her standing by your wardrobe shirtless; your clothes scattered around her feet like petals—her first transgression.

Nearer to the end, you'd wonder if Mama Lateef had also been right about this other thing: whether girls like Joy were quick to forget. And whether or not she had been right, it would already be too late. By the time Joy would commit her second transgression, you'd had your child, a pretty boy who would grow up to cause the women of the world much trouble. You had him a few minutes past one a.m. in May; a boy with his umbilical wrapped around his neck, a boy the unique circumstances of whose birth would compel you to give him the oriki "Aina," long before it was decided that Sesan would be his first name. And though you never told Yinka, you had thought that the baby would never make it, that he'd enter the world as a pool of blood. It was what the woman in your dreams had told you, the one who pestered you every night until you told her a story. And so many did you tell her—folktales, urban myths from your childhood, the salacious love stories that colored your secondary school years, and awful summaries of your book club readings—until you believed you had run out of stories. And then she reminded you that you had one more: the story about your son, how he never makes it out of the maternity ward, how he dies before being born because nothing survives women like you.

You blamed the book *Joys of Motherhood* for your nightmares, for it was while reading it that the nightmares began. And you were not alone: so strong a hold did the novel take on your book club that, thenceforth, the discussions were sober and somber, as though a wreath of clouds had appeared around your group. Things may have worsened when Jumoke, who gave birth—as she had predicted—before the club could discuss the novel, lost her baby to pneumonia less than a day after arriving home from the hospital. Nneka called you to break the news and not in her usual way, not katikati, but delicately. And the next evening, Bola called you to say book club meetings had been temporarily suspended and, before ending the call, warned you about your girl.

"Some of those girls are bad luck," she said. Hers, for instance, had been telling Peju, Bola's husband, *things*. "And Jumoke," she added, "confronted her house girl in a dream before losing her child."

You would ask Bola to calm down, to be reasonable, not expecting the deluge of confessions that followed.

She asked, "Are you alone? Do you have time to talk?"

You would leave your bedroom and respond, "Bola, you're scaring me." And during the rest of the phone call that seemed your longest yet, you would learn not only of Bola's husband's impotence, but also of the many things women do to remain women.

Joy's second transgression took its time before it occurred, and when it happened, it didn't catch you off guard. Rather, it left you feeling the girl had intended for you to discover that particular offense easily. And there was motive: only a few days after you had given birth, Joy came to you requesting permission to leave school for good. She had felt it would be better (for her mostly) if, instead of going to school, she trained to be a seamstress, learned a trade among people her age. She had found a seamstress who was willing to train her and you knew this woman, Rasheeda, whose studio was right across the street. Rasheeda had sewn every aṣọ-ẹbi you had bought since you and Yinka started living in Surulere.

It was June when Joy came to you with her plan: she promised she'd stay in school until the term ended in July; the last thing she wanted was to seem ungrateful or for Mama Lateef to brand her a waste, an oniranu, should you take Joy's suggestion the wrong way and send her back to the old woman. Joy was shocked when you barely looked at her and said no; when you told her you were, as a matter of fact, relieved she no longer wanted to go to school because you needed her at home to watch the baby. She nodded when you told her you would be returning to work very soon, and replied, "Yes, ma, okay, ma."

It took you until Christmas that year, your second Christmas with Joy, to realize the following changes the girl had undergone: first was her English, which no longer had gaps and creases but was smooth enough for Yinka to notice and even ask you about it. But you dismissed it then as nothing important. She was learning from television, you had explained to Yinka. Now that she stayed at home with the baby, she spent a great deal of time watching films, mostly Nigerian, sometimes Indian, and it was only natural that she pick up a few phrases. If her reading had improved too, it was because the Indian films required she be able to understand the subtitles.

After her English, you started noticing the way she smelled: like you. That is, like you after your usual spritz of Terry Mugler's Angel, one on each side of your neck. It violated you, the thought of her creeping over your belongings (once, you could accept as an error, but again and again?); it made you ransack your dressing table, counting your creams, perfume bottles, and lotions, but none, it appeared, was missing. And locking your bedroom had no impact. Still, sometimes you felt your wigs had been tampered with; sometimes your clothes (bras especially) felt warm, ill-fitting, as though someone else had been in them. And then, the crown of all changes was how Joy no longer buried her laughter in your presence but sounded ebullient. How her laughter bloomed, percolated, and spread bold colors. How even from your bedroom upstairs, you could hear her. And always it stunned you to find her downstairs, with Yinka at the root of her laughter.

You suspected whatever it was between Joy and Yinka began on Christmas Eve that December, the year everything changed. Yinka, who had been the branch manager of a bank in Ikeja, had called you one evening the first week of that very month, claiming he was on his way home.

"Why?" you had asked. It was too early; you hadn't even started cooking; was he feeling well? He had been complaining to you about migraines; was he driving? Could he make sure he was careful? The worst things happen around the end of the year. Yinka would explain that he was fired that morning *(no,* you'd respond); his bank *(no)*, which had just been acquired by a bigger bank, was *(no, no, no, no)* restructuring; many banks, you knew, had been restructuring since 2005. The banks were too small in terms of how much money they held as capital, Yinka had told you back then, and because he didn't want to bore you with the details, papapa, he had summarized that the Nationwide Recapitalization Program would be good for everyone.

"Trust me," he had said. As he wept over the phone, you remembered how smug he had been telling you about Nigerian banks that year, how proud he was because he believed in his bank, and how proud you were of him because nobody needed to tell you that your Yinka was an astute banker, one of the best.

Even when, months before you hired Joy, he told you that a much bigger bank was planning to acquire his bank, when he confessed that he feared they'd let him go if the acquisition fell through, you had told him, "Let you of all people go, kẹ? Those are fears of sheep and I married a leopard. Ko possible. End of story."

But not only was it possible, it happened. Yinka was fired that December. And Yinka wilted in unemployment, he shriveled, might as well have swallowed himself—in other words, o ru. You had decided to put your savings into retail and had made the final payment for a store on Bode Thomas, where you would sell children's clothes imported from the US, and the months that followed were the most difficult yet. In those months, you felt the entire weight of your marriage shift toward your side. Sometimes, as you lay together at night, you would ask Yinka how things were going, whether things were going to be better, wanting him to say yes. But Yinka would never respond. All you knew was that he was looking for a job, and that he was getting tired of it. You would face your side of the bedroom, your back against his, and sigh.

And then one night, you asked again how he was feeling and as you turned away ignored, you heard him say: "You had no right to withdraw that girl from school."

Ọlọrun, you swore to yourself, *that girl will not kill me.*

* * *

The film was *Kabhi Khushi Kabhie Gham* and you were the only one in Lagos who hadn't seen it. You had asked your salesgirl, Kemi, to buy a copy as she left for Ola Iya, the nearest canteen to your store, where she bought lunch for your favorite customers. The boys who hawked films always swarmed that area. It was Bola from your still-defunct book club—who since you opened the store had become one such customer—that recommended the film. She owned a beauty salon in Akerele that was famous for its stock of Indian films and was surprised when you told her you had never heard of it.

On Christmas Eve, you walked into your living room while the film was playing. You still hadn't watched it, but you recognized the soundtrack, which the girls at Bola's salon overplayed. That evening, you arrived home from your shop to a house that smelled of your signature perfume, and a front door that had been left unlocked, as if for you. You could hear laughter, a commingling of voices. You feared the worst was happening and stormed into the living room to meet Yinka, laid out on the sofa, laughing, and Joy, seated on the ground across the sofa, laughing too. She saw you and greeted, "Welcome, ma." She no longer hid her face when she spoke to you and you were still very unfamiliar with this renewed Joy. She even looked at you as if she was searching for traces of panic and enjoying it.

"Go and bring the things from the car," you said to her, your voice scattered, eyes darting. "Where is Sesan?"

She responded: "Baby is sleeping, ma." And when she walked past you heading for the door, you swore she meant to lean toward you, because you smelled it all over her. Yes, your perfume, but that wasn't even it, the ọdaju-eyan wasn't wearing any underwear. She stank of lust.

* * *

You never discussed Christmas Eve with Yinka. You simply weren't sure, still had your doubts. Premature confrontation was for women in Yoruba films and you were more pragmatic than that. The only time you had tried to tell Yinka that there was something odd about Joy, he looked at you strangely, having never forgiven you for removing the girl from school, having threatened you about sending her back to Mama Lateef, yelling, "Haven't you done enough?" Besides, you don't just wake up and accuse your husband of sleeping with the house girl because what if he says that he did? What then? O-hoo. And you knew Yoruba men owned up to much worse.

You tried taking the matter to God. You followed Bola, whose issues with her husband seemed to have been miraculously resolved, to three prophets, one of whom was an ẹlẹmi that assured you the Devil was in your house.

"The Devil," the elemi said in tongues the other prophets translated, "wants all that is yours. The Devil covets and when you have lost everything, the Devil, being insatiable, will come for you." Bisi, ṣọ ara ẹ. La oju ẹ! The prophets wanted to know if you had been having strange dreams and you told them of the woman you sometimes dreamed of, who by this time had some stories of her own. You told them how now the woman in your dreams wanted you to listen to her own stories, how you had never seen the woman's face, never mind the many times you had tried to steal a glance. You never mentioned Christmas Eve, never mentioned how, on several occasions since then, you had caught Joy glaring at you, and how, each time, you had felt like something about to be eaten. You only listened as they told you what special prayers they would make on your behalf and wrote down their instructions for your part in this battle against Satan: *Light one abẹla each day of the week for seven weeks; mark what is yours with anointed oil; cover all mirrors; read Psalms 27 and 109 first thing every morning and last thing every night; gbadura! Gbadura!*

And you would have put your heart into each and every one of these things had they seemed dependable, had you not closed your heart to God long before you even met Yinka, and if prayer didn't turn to dust in your mouth whenever you tried to call on Him. You remembered that in the Nollywood films both you and Joy used to watch, justice arrived on the heels of crimes—if not immediately, eventually. The question, then, was should you simply wait for your justice to arrive? Throughout your life, you had watched women like Patience Ozokwor play villains, and seen that villains were always vanquished, but you also knew that the Hilda Dokubos of Nigerian cinema played scorned, tortured women who always outlived their malefactors but were never duly compensated. Always. Where on that spectrum would Joy place herself? Where would she place you? Did she consider these things as she tormented you?

You believed justice according to Nigerian films was clumsy, neither fair nor meaningful, always lax on villains: all one really needed to do was confess her crimes and next were the credits and To God Be the Glory. But that did not mean such films were false; in fact, you were banking on the inevitability of getting away with whatever it was you were going to do to Joy. If you looked hard enough, wouldn't you see that everyone who was anyone in Lagos was a villain in some way? You were going to trade places with Joy, take control of the script, give Hilda the juju for once, and let Patience mourn. You wanted it that way so that when people tell this story, because they always will, listeners will find it difficult to imagine you. In their minds, you'd transcend that spectrum, being neither a typical Patience nor a Hilda and nowhere in between. There are three kinds of women, and the third, you swore, was your kind—an Ijebu woman defending her house, the kind of woman to go after what was hers, the kind to hold no regrets over whatever she does to remain a woman, the kind who never lost.

Once you defined being such a woman as contingent on Joy suffering, there was no stopping you. It was like hearing the voice of God, and nothing had ever sounded as fulfilling, reassuring, or sweet. The moment that voice came to you, you abandoned the prophets for more practical instruments. Then you waited: for the right price, the right amount, for night to arrive, for Yinka to fall asleep, and then for Joy to fall asleep. Once you were certain your conditions had been met, you walked to her bedroom, where Joy slept under air-conditioning and on a foam mattress wrapped in cotton sheets—excesses the result of unnecessary kindness. You had five liters of sulphuric acid in a keg you were going to douse over her like a gardener tending her hedges, until every drop had been assigned a patch of skin. So you opened the door and crept into her bedroom. The room was unlit but you could make out her bed by the window; just outside in the sky hung a sickle moon. You called out to her softly, "Joy, Joy," and when there was no response you were sure she was fast asleep. It gladdened you. Carelessly, hands shaking, you unscrewed the keg. You held it over her bed and screamed when the door opened behind you with a bang. It was Joy in the doorway and the bed was vacant, just a bunch of pillows that had more than deceived you. She terrified you when she opened the door, and you dropped the keg. You could hear its contents spilling over the ground, singeing the carpet.

"Mummy," she sometimes called you this, "ṣ'ẹn wa mi?"

You stormed out of her bedroom.

"Emi ree," she said as you ran to your own room. "Mummy!" she screamed after you. She was on to you. If not that night, one day the ẹlẹmi-eṣu would come for you.

It was a week before Easter, your third year with Joy, when Yinka got a job interview in Abuja. He didn't dwell on the details, having gone for numerous interviews already, all of which had been unsuccessful; he wanted to temper his hopes. It was an impromptu interview for a managerial position at a telecom company with several offices in Lagos. In Abuja he'd be meeting with the executive director of the company at a conference. It was a once-in-a-lifetime opportunity, you had heard him tell someone over the phone. The way he spoke, he could have been referring to either the interview or the job.

At first, you didn't want him to leave you in Lagos, not with that girl, not with Joy. But you knew how important the interview was to him, and so in the morning on the day he was set to leave, you made him promise to come back home that very night. He explained that flights between Lagos and Abuja were unpredictable and unreliable, but you made him swear he would try. He wanted to know why you were frightened; he confessed to you, as a way of easing you, that he had a good feeling about this particular interview: his former boss had recommended him, had reached out to the ED on his behalf. Things were about to change for the better. But ki lo dẹ de? He wondered why his saying all of that had not put your mind at rest. You told him not to worry, he wouldn't understand. Things had been strange for a while between the two of you and he wanted to talk once he got back, *to smooth things over* were the words he used. You realized that he meant this sincerely and it occurred to you then that Christmas Eve could have been a lie, something Joy put together to throw you off-balance. It felt unfamiliar as you said it but you told Yinka that you loved him, and although he looked perplexed he said he loved you too. You wanted to tell him everything then, about that night with Joy, the keg of acid, how she cackled as you ran back to your room, but instead you wished him a safe flight and asked him to call you once he had landed. He said he'd tell you all about the interview when he got home that night.

"Ṣe iyẹn wa okay?" he asked, teasing you with the present tense. It was the happiest you had seen him in a while.

"Ẹhn mo ti gbọ," you replied. Just come back home tonight.

Ever since that night with Joy, you kept your distance from her. That was what Bola, the only person you shared your fears with, advised. On Joy's part, you explained to Bola, she acted as though that night had never happened and this only made her more sinister, an ẹlẹmi-eṣu, true-true. As soon as Yinka left for the airport, you decided that no longer was Joy going to be allowed anywhere near you and your family. You moved her things to an old room behind the house, so that she would no longer sleep inside the same building as you. Unsatisfied, you called Mama Lateef, telling yourself you didn't care if it would upset Yinka; men, you and Bola had agreed, never understand these things until it's too late. Even when Mama Lateef tried to persuade you to take another girl, you let her know that you had had one house girl too many, though you never explained what you meant.

All you said was, "We don't know where these girls are from, who they are, what animosities they carry inside of them; we can never really know. Yet we invite them into our lives, we leave them with our babies, we let them cook for us, claim we can trust them—what if they turn out to be bad people?"

"Joy isn't a bad girl," Mama Lateef said. She insisted she knew the girl. At the last place she worked, the children refused to eat if Joy wasn't around; she brought the parents so much luck they would have paid triple the amount you paid to keep her, but it was Joy who left. "Joy likes you. Mi o mọ reason ti o fi like yin, but she does. She said to me, the first time she saw you, that she must live with you. She thinks you are the most beautiful woman she has ever seen." At this, Mama Lateef laughed. "Ṣe yẹn wa jọ ọmọ buruku? Haba!"

You decided you couldn't blame Mama Lateef for Joy, you made it clear you blamed yourself, all of it was your own fault, you who had enabled a society in which girls like Joy were forced to exist, you who had once relished such a society.

"Ẹ ma binu," you told Mama Lateef finally. "We just think we can manage by ourselves. We don't want Joy anymore." And you looked forward to Easter Sunday, when Mama Lateef was coming to take her away.

That evening, you got a call from Yinka. He wanted you to know that his interview had been moved to the following day, which meant he wouldn't be able to make it home that night. You were standing by the window, watching the children in the compound next door. They were playing Catcher. All day, there had been no light at home and you told Yinka what you had learned that afternoon, that the generator that powered your house had packed up. Your security guard had blamed the diesel on which the generator had been running. He claimed the diesel that had been in the house was a bad batch that had been mixed, it seemed, with kerosene. Most likely the person who sold the diesel had tampered with it. As a result, the engine, he said, had knocked. You told Yinka the guard had been out all evening looking for a mechanic. Yinka groaned over the phone but you had an odd feeling that things were going to be fine. You felt strangely lightheaded and the horizon had never seemed so promising. So you told Yinka not to worry; to focus on his interview; this time next year the two of you would be looking back with Sesan—Sesan, you suddenly wondered, where was he? "Hold on," you told Yinka. You walked over to the other end of your bedroom, to Sesan's cot, and he wasn't there. You searched your own bed, threw the sheets across the room, and your baby wasn't there. He wasn't across the corridor in Yinka's study. He wasn't downstairs in the living room or in the room that was formerly Joy's (you went downstairs because he was crawling now, and you knew he wasn't good at climbing stairs yet, so you hoped he hadn't tried to and failed). It wasn't until you left your bedroom that you realized you could smell smoke, and only when you arrived downstairs did you see the smoke was coming from the kitchen. You ran there, opened the door, and the backdraft sent you crashing into the cabinet where you kept some porcelain ornaments. You ran to the front door, already screaming for help, but the front door, too, was locked. So you dashed upstairs to your bedroom, evading the fire, but for how long?

Back in your bedroom, your phone was on the windowsill, propped against the burglary-proof bars that separated you from the window's glass. Yinka was asking: "Bisi, are you there?"

You ran to the phone, meaning to respond, but something in the other compound caught your attention. It was Joy, playing Catcher with the other children. She was holding your son against her waist; your son, whose first word, you remembered, had been her name. The children stopped playing for it had become obvious that the house next door to them was burning. Then they started running, shouting, "Fire! Fire!" All except Joy, who knew your window and stood glaring at it, at you. She stood there, watching. On her index finger was a key ring and affixed to that ring, a bunch of kcys you watched Sesan playing with idly. You didn't even have time.

"Joy," you screamed. "My baby! Joy!" All that came to you while screaming was that September when Joy stood in that same bedroom half-naked, when she showed you who she was and you thought it safer to doubt her. You tore your lungs weeping as people gathered to watch your house, hands tucked underneath their arms, heads shaking, mouthing, *Omaṣe o.*

Is this me? you wondered. *Is this my life?* By the time you remembered your phone, Yinka was saying, "Never mind, I'll call you later. Darling, I have to go."

PART III

ARRIVALS & DEPARTURES

CHOIR BOY

BY 'PEMI AGUDA
Berger

You want to know the story of the woman who cradles her naked breasts and thrusts them into the faces of strangers? *Madwoman,* you call her. But what do *you* know?

You want to know if hers is the story of the grieving mother: the mother whose baby entered the world quiet and blue and too well behaved to be alive. If her breasts became so heavy with milk that her mind broke, snapped so badly that she offers her dead baby's milk to anyone who will have it.

No, that is not her story.

Okay, now you're asking if hers is the story of a woman so consumed by her own vanity that she turned every man away. If it is the story of a spurned suitor who spoke a sentence to two sticks at three in the morning and caused her brain to scramble. And now maybe she begs every man on the street to look at her big brown nipples and fall back in love.

But you're wrong again, that's not her story.

I'll tell you her story. But first I have to tell you *my* story. I am not happy to tell it, but everything is connected. Isn't every story dependent on another story? Isn't everything connected?

Please be patient, I will tell you *my* story. Then I will tell you hers.

* * *

It was one of those Friday nights when that big church had their monthly services. The roads were blocked as usual. I sat in that danfo with as many people as the conductor could convince to enter—they were up to six in one row. We were headed to Berger, where my own church was having a night program for the choir members. *Mm-hmm,* I was a chorister.

No, not anymore. But I am coming to that. Calm down, please. You are the one who has asked for the woman's story. Every story is connected.

I used to sing so beautifully that many people cried. I would stand on that elevated sacred stage with the purple carpet, and as I opened my throat and let the sounds caress the microphone in worship, the people would look up at me, eyes wide and glazed, tears rolling down either side of their open mouths like brackets. It is the closest I have ever felt to a god.

But that night, stuck between a smallish woman, unnervingly still, and a snoring man, I could feel the frustrations of the whole bus. It was palpable in the humid night air hanging over us in that dark bus. The lights from the phone screens reflected on the exposed metal roof and played tricks on my tired eyes. People sighed, hissed, and cursed Lagos, the church, the air, and even their parents for birthing them in Nigeria.

I wasn't as bothered as most on the bus; I was going to be early for my program no matter how long we were stuck in traffic. My plan was to get to church early, pray for an hour, then practice some new songs before others started coming in. Let me tell you, my friend—things aren't always as they should be, you know? See, whenever I got off that stage in church, I became regular. I don't understand it. Segun, who didn't make anyone cry when he sang, whose alto sounded like a broken blender—he was the choir director. He was the one fucking all the tenor girls.

I'm sorry; I don't mean to shock you. I'm just saying it as it is. How did I know? Well, because I am—was—that guy who all the girls confided in. The one who goes unnoticed in the corner of the room until someone else breaks their heart and then they realize, *Oh, this one has the perfect shoulder to receive my tears, and his ears are just small enough to hear my secrets and keep them in.*

I'm not distracted, I'm getting there! I'm coming to it. You should know everything is layered, don't ask for an abridged version—you owe it to the story.

So, everyone was tense and uncomfortable in that sardine tin of a bus. It smelled too, like the sweat and exhaustion of the whole week. Nobody complained when the driver decided to try a short cut, a corner-corner road beside Road Safety. You know it? No, the one after the filling station. Yes, that one.

Anyway, it was that fat policewoman sitting in front who suggested it. So, even if we had to pass a one-way to get there, she was going to be our golden ticket. Or can police arrest police in Lagos?

Can you tell when you are about to enter trouble? Can you? Me, I can't. Even when I had that accident last week, it was because I didn't see the okada coming. Everyone asked me: "How were you hit by an ordinary okada when you could have jumped out of the way?" I have no answer. I think my survival instincts go numb instead of peaking when danger is around.

Anyway, the conductor jumped out of the bus and directed the driver away from the crawling thread of cars. The gap we created was quickly filled by other hungry vehicles. Even when the smallish woman tensed further, folding herself closer into her body as if trying hard to make no contact, my senses were not triggered. And when the snoring man jerked awake, I assumed it was the sudden increase in speed. I went back to my phone.

It wasn't until the first person demanded to know how the street we were on linked to Berger; until the conductor jabbed his elbow into the man who tried to reach around him to open the door; it wasn't till we pulled onto the dirt road with no lights that my hands started to shake.

Suddenly, the bus was full of noise. There were many plaintive cries to Jesus and Allah, and some to the driver and conductor. Someone demanded that the policewoman do something but she stayed quiet. So quiet.

Everything happened quickly after that. I started to text someone—anyone—to tell them I was being abducted, but the bus had swung into a compound. Figures appeared from the shadows to lock the gate behind us. I did not feel like it was quite happening to me yet, it was too surreal—like I was watching a bad Nollywood movie.

And then there were guns and many men yanking us out of the bus. Shaking a bucket in our faces: *Drop your phones, drop your phones.* Nokias and iPhones and HTCs fell into the plastic bucket amidst *Hello?* and *Ha, what's happening here, is someone screaming?*

I let mine go easily.

We were under a large tree with a single floodlight directed downward. It looked like the setting for an outdoor play. I could see the policewoman more clearly then. She was wide. The buttons of her black shirt barely held her breasts inside. The gaps between each button were shadowy ellipses. I turned away. I wondered if she was a real policewoman gone rogue, or an imposter. Those uniforms are so easy to imitate, you know?

"Officer?" the conductor called out to her from the entrance of the bus.

She cocked her head toward some building and headed there herself. I tried to squint past the tree, past the darkness that withheld the rest of the compound from my eyes—but nothing. We were forced into a queue and directed toward the building. Two buff men started to pat us down and check our bags for valuables. I saw more phones, iPads, and other devices I didn't recognize. There was a bottle of wine. Another man stood behind, collecting bank cards and asking us to write down our PINs.

The queue moved slowly. I tried to make a mental list of all the items in my bag. Some woman in front of me had tried to do a physical appraisal of her bag's contents and got slapped by the driver, who had now joined the party. He was a tall man who walked stooped over; he had a toothpick hanging from his mouth. He never said a word.

My Bible. My song notepad. Some music sheets. My wallet. About two thousand naira? Two bank cards—one empty, the other still bursting with my administrative assistant salary that had been paid only the week before.

I had the time of four people ahead of me to decide if I was ready to part with my money by giving them the correct PIN.

But what if they hurt us if they found out we lied?

Then there were three people between me and a decision.

I tried to peep behind the officer and bouncers to see if there was anyone with a gun. I hadn't seen any yet, and I didn't know whether to be pacified or terrified of the unknown.

She was staring at me, the officer.

I turned away from her eyes. They were dark slits above swells of fair round cheeks. Then there was one person.

She was still staring at me.

I am not a manly looking man, as you can see. My shoulders aren't wide enough, my mustache won't grow past these sketchy strands, and I'm only five-seven. Is that why the choir girls preferred Segun to me? Who knows? The officer was staring at me as if I was more than this skinny person who was doing everything to avoid her gaze.

Then I was standing before the trio. The first man gently took my bag from me. I still didn't look up. I studied the black tennis shoes of Thug A and the peeling leather of Thug B's boots.

"What's your name?" I didn't answer immediately. The officer's voice was raspy but soft, like something was pressing down her throat. Maybe fat.

"You no hear Officer?"

I stuttered, said my name. I still didn't look up.

I moved on to the next man, who collected my bank cards; I wrote down the correct PIN.

The space was bare terrazzo floors and peeling paint on brown walls that opened to glassless windows. Wooden benches sat in rows and we filled them one by one after being stripped of our belongings. The silent roof yawned above us, with its exposed beams and creaking iron sheets. Five fluorescent tubes stuck to the beams lit up the space; a sixth one blinked loudly, causing my eyes to twitch.

To an outsider we would have looked like people waiting for their driver's licenses at a government office. Except for the occasional moan, whimper, or burst of prayer, we would have passed. I was back beside the still woman. She stared straight ahead with her arms around her chest. I hoped she was all right.

And then we waited. We heard two bikes rev and leave the compound, to the ATMs, I assumed. They left behind a cricket-filled silence that bore down on us from the darkness outside. My pulse played a wild beat in my neck. I kept my gaze level with the sweat-stained brown collar of the man in front of me.

And then the officer called out my name. I froze before I twisted to the back. The still woman finally turned to stare at me in confusion. *I'm not one of them,* I wanted so badly to clarify to her gentle brown eyes. *She just asked for my name!* Instead I turned my head slowly toward the exit.

"Me?"

"You."

I held my lighter bag in my hand as I bumped against the knees of my fellow abductees to get out to the aisle.

"What is that in your bag?"

My heartbeat doubled, if that was possible. I started to worry that I had somehow managed to hide something from them.

My neck went hot. "Wh-what?"

Her hand pointed to the bag. Her wrist and fingers were so tiny, out of proportion with the rest of her. Like someone had tied a rubber band there to prevent the fat from seeping into her hands. I looked from the bag to her hand.

"Ma?"

Yes, so I was a timid man, still am depending on the situation. Have you ever been stared down by a huge policewoman with one tiny hand in her trouser pockets and the other pointing at your bag?

I opened the bag and peered inside. She reached over herself and pulled out my music sheets. "This."

"Oh," I sighed, "it's just music."

"Music?"

"Yes, ma." Sweat slid down my neck to glide down my spine. My T-shirt stuck to it.

"You're a musician?" She leaned back against the doorless frame.

"No, ma, I'm a chorister."

"For church?"

"Yes, ma."

She gestured for me to follow her outside the building. I trailed her around to the side with no windows. I missed the light.

"So you sing in church?" She was leaning against the wall. I could no longer see her clearly, just a dark outline of a sinister mass.

"Yes, ma."

"Choir?"

"Yes, ma."

"Shey, your God will forgive us for this one we don do tonight?"

Who was I to preach repentance to a woman who held my safety in her tiny hands? I nodded, mute.

"Oya, sing for me." The request was whispered. I pretended not to hear. I took a tiny step backward.

"Oya. Sing for me." It was louder this time. No longer a request. A demand.

"I . . . I can't sing, ma."

I didn't think there was space but she reached behind her to pull a small gun from her waistband. This was my first time seeing a gun up close. It glinted dully in the little light it could catch. Then I felt it against my skin, smack in the middle of my forehead.

"Oya, choir boy, I said sing for me."

My mouth opened and closed. I swallowed air, coughed it out. Then: "*In Christ alone my hope is found; He is my light, my strength, my song . . .*"

I stared down at my leather slippers, at the dust, at a new wound on the little toe of my right foot.

The officer moved her gun to tip my chin back up. I was forced to look at her, to survey her forehead, gleaming with sweat; her nose, wide and oily; her tiny eyes, beady things squinting at me; her big lips, painted in flaky brown, curled up to one side.

"*This cornerstone, this solid ground, firm through the fiercest drought and storm* . . ." My voice was small, my notes halting as they left my mouth. *Don't think of church, don't think of the altar,* I told myself. "*What heights of love, what depths of peace* . . ."

And then her other hand rose to my waist. It raised my T-shirt up, her hand grazing my jutting pelvic bone. She moved the gun back to my forehead and then she tucked a hand into a belt loop and pulled me forward. I closed my eyes. She did not prompt me to open them.

"*When fears are stilled, when strivings cease* . . ."

She unbuckled my belt with one hand. Then she yanked my penis into her grip. I was limp all over. I swallowed air; I couldn't sing anymore. Her hands were sweaty against me. I swallowed air again. I swallowed nothing. I pinched my eyes shut tighter.

Her gun tapped my chin again. "Finish your song."

"*My comforter, my all in all* . . . *Here in the love of Christ I stand.*"

She stood there with her eyes closed, working on my thing slowly with her lips turned up in that way. I wanted to bash her skull into the wall behind; watch it splatter. But there was that gun and there was me—the skinny timid man whose shoulder the choir girls cry on after fucking Segun.

Is it still worship if the ears that hear it belong to a criminal? If the eyes that drift shut at its sound belong to this woman with her hands down my trousers?

She let go of me suddenly, as if disgusted by my lack of response. She tucked her gun back into her waistband and stalked away. Her gait was a horizontal sway, one heavy tread after the other. I tidied myself and started to walk back, hesitantly, to join the others. I wondered if they'd heard me singing. I realized I had tears on my cheeks when I saw the stooped driver cocking his head at me. The policewoman didn't look at me again.

They let us go eventually. The people who gave the correct PINs were put into the bus and dropped off at Berger. I don't know what happened to the other people; my still neighbor was one of them. The traffic had cleared by then, and I went straight to church where I sat in the back and cried all through the program. Everyone thought it was the Holy Ghost.

I'm only telling you this so you will understand what it did to me. Yes, I have come to her story. It is a short one, but you need to remember how this episode had affected me—I couldn't sing in church anymore without remembering slimy hands against a flaccid cock. So I left.

Yes, I've gotten to it.

It was past eleven p.m. another night—slightly over a year after my . . . you know, the episode. I was only just starting to relax again in night buses.

You ask me why I didn't stop taking buses? Ah, what could I do? Nothing. There are no options for a poor man. Poor man has to work; poor man cannot afford to live on the island; poor man closes really late. I had to suffer through the journeys, my butt clenched so hard on the thin pads that did nothing to cushion against the metal frames. Peering at every passenger for a sign of duplicity.

Anyway, I was in a bus heading toward Yaba from Obalende. We'd gotten to that stretch of road that ramps off the Third Mainland Bridge. The only street where lights repel the police and attract hooligans? The one people speed past because of all the horror stories? Well, we didn't go fast enough for this story. The robbers stopped us with the tires that littered the road, so close to our destination.

It was the night I almost pissed my pants when I saw a gun for the second time. And this woman was sitting beside me, and she trembled and I trembled. We all trembled. It must have been a slow night for them to be stopping a danfo. The road yawned empty and ominous before and behind us.

They knocked the bus conductor unconscious because all his bus stop bravado had been reduced to a murmuring mess of Yoruba gibberish. One of them had the driver lying flat under his foot. The other three asked us to bring out our phones, bags, and money. I was seated in the row directly behind the conductor and it didn't take many whimpers and growls before it was my turn. I handed over my cheap Nokia, familiar with the routine.

And then the one with the long fingernail on his pinkie saw her. He had a knife, and I remember thinking it was quite fancy with its decorated handle of gleaming stones. But the curve and glint of the knife laid any illusions of fancy to waste. He pointed the knife at her, then jerked it to point outside. She obeyed. I had to clamber out of my window seat so she could pass. I admit that I immediately plastered myself against the bus to try to render myself invisible.

Then, with the knife resting on her collarbone, I saw him rip her blouse open. It was a loose floral shirt that was cut high. But she had those breasts that would announce themselves even in a nun's habit. I am indicted by the memory of watching them jiggle over the bumps in the road that night.

The ripping sound was loud. She stepped back, recoiling. The man raised the heavy handle of the knife and hit her head with a dull thump. She whimpered and stood still. His gang paused to look at him, clearly surprised at this twist. One chuckled and called him an *omo ale*—bastard. Pulling breasts out of her lacy navy-blue bra, he lowered his head and took a nipple into his mouth.

I remember his shirt, you see. It was one of those green *My Money Grows Like Grass* tees. I remember his neck; it was strained at that angle—I could see his spine pressing out of his sweaty skin. I remember the silence.

Oh, it was silent. I couldn't stop looking from between my fingers. No, don't look at me that way. I couldn't. Was it the horror that had me frozen? I don't know. Maybe I wanted to see if she would handle it differently than I had? But then, she had a bigger audience.

It was silent except for his suckling and little moans. Everyone stayed quiet as he moved from left to right, and right to left. The blood trickled down her face from the skin his knife had split below her hairline.

It is because I couldn't stop looking that I saw when she left her body behind. Her eyes went blank, my friend. There was nothing left in her dark irises. And that was when I turned away. Another woman in the bus began to cry loudly. It was as if they shared the same spirit and she was the one who could weep.

Nobody cried for me.

I remember the sound. It still sits at the back of my neck. It was one lady, but I swear she sounded like a whole village of mourning women. It came out of her and the robbers snapped back to action.

They took our money and our bags and our voices.

After they sped off on their bikes, the other women gathered around the victim. They tucked her breasts away and gave her their scarves to cover the shreds of her blouse, but she did not say a word. I have never heard a silence so scary.

And then a man laughed. I don't remember which. He laughed and slapped his thigh and shook his head.

The laughter seemed to provoke something in her. She brushed the women aside and went to him. She put her hands underneath her breasts, cupped them, and pushed toward him.

"Go on. Finish it. Kill me." And the laughter did not stop. Yes, it was me.

I couldn't stop laughing: at the idea that covering her breasts would somehow cloak the memory; at the idea that after tonight, she wouldn't wake up every night feeling the slobbery slipperiness of a stranger's tongue under her shirt. I laughed at the foolishness.

The driver recovered and the conductor was shaken awake. They asked everyone to get back in, but she didn't. We left her behind, pushing her breasts toward the bus as she became smaller, and grainier, and unidentifiable through the dusty rear window of the bus.

There she is now. And this is her story that you wanted to know.

THE WALKING STICK

BY E.C. OSONDU

Agege

They found the body in the early afternoon, just when the children from the infant classes were coming back from school. They let the toddlers out early so that they could have their lunches before they became too hungry. If he had not died, he would have been in his favorite bar in the camp, holding a bottle of his favorite lager beer—33 Export—by the scruff of the neck, and calling the returning schoolchildren by the special nicknames he had for each one of them as they ran home.

"Ma wife, ah dis no good-o you not even wan greet ya husband today. Ha, my wife no good-o," he would say to one of the little girls returning from school.

To another a boy with a big belly he would call out: "Big belly boy! See how your belly big, and you neva start to drink beer yet. When you start to drink beer your belly will be bigger than this drum." Then he would point at the big red drum filled with a block of ice and beer bottles that shivered as they rested on their freezing bed.

Usually after his third bottle of 33 Export he would start dancing. By this time, the older children would be on their way back from school. He had no cute exchange with these ones, and he dared not give them cute nicknames. As he danced, they mocked him—they called *him* names. These were tough kids. Life in the Refugee Resettlement Center off the Agric bus stop in Agege was rough, and even at this age they had seen quite a few of the cruel ways that life could slash and cut people up, children included.

"Drunkard man, see how he is dancing like his legs are broken," one of the schoolboys said one afternoon, and they all began to laugh. They had already learned how to make their wretched lives more bearable by making others feel even more miserable.

"Tell him to buy us 7UP," one of them urged their leader.

"Drunkard man, c'mon, buy us 7UP," the leader of the group demanded. He was not begging; his voice was hard.

The man held out his half-empty bottle of 33 Export. They shook their heads. They were hungry, and beer would only make them feel even more famished. They wanted 7UP. They could imagine its cold, filtered sweetness flowing down their throats into their bellies. Was it his offer of beer that made them angry? Seemingly from nowhere, a certain cruelty crept into them, and they picked up stones and began throwing them violently at the man. He stopped dancing and yelled when a rock came close to hitting him. He clutched the beer to his chest, cradling it as if saving the bottle was more important. The woman who owned the drinking shack ran out with a broom and chased after the children until they fled. "Useless children!" she yelled after them.

The next day on their way home from school, the boys were looking forward to another interlude at the bar—they liked the entertainment—but the man with the drink was not there. As they stood outside the shack looking for him, the woman who ran the bar came out. That was when she realized that something unusual had happened: the man who would usually be on his third bottle of 33 Export lager was not there.

Where was he? Why was he not at her bar drinking? Was he at another bar?

No, hers was the man's favorite bar in the camp. He could not have risked leaving the camp and going into town to drink. The owners of the bars in town were not Liberians, and they did not like the Liberian refugees, even though they liked their money and their girls.

The man was not at her bar drinking today because he was dead.

Dead men do not drink 33 Export lager.

Sergeant Joseph Gorewa was sitting at his desk in the Isokoko police station in Agege, trying his best to think. This was an impossible task, considering that the police station was right beside the ever-noisy Agege Market and also opposite the railway tracks. There was a saying that if you could not find something at Agege Market, you wouldn't be able to find it anywhere in Lagos. If there was ever a break in the constant din from the market, it would be interrupted by the shrill whistle of an approaching locomotive train, belching smoke, with passengers perched like locusts on every part of it.

Joseph Gorewa had many things on his mind. At this moment, though, he was thinking about the act of thinking. He wondered how it was possible that as soon as one thought exited his mind, another followed. How was it that the mind could have all these thoughts and not burst?

But one thought was persistently crowding out the rest: how could he make his pay last beyond two weeks? No matter how much he tried, he could never make his take-home pay last to the end of the month. He was thinking that there must be some way to be more frugal. Perhaps he could stop making calls and start only sending messages because they cost less.

He had tried it once, but each time he sent his wife a text message she would text him back saying, *Call me now.* Perhaps this was a strategy he needed to try again.

At that moment his phone rang. It was his boss; the DPO. Joe Gorewa stood up and saluted as he took the call. He could never take a call from his boss while seated. No matter how much he planned to, on every occasion he would find his legs forcing themselves upright and his hand shooting out in a salute.

"There has been a homicide at the Refugee Resettlement Center by the Agric bus stop. You must go there immediately. These are refugees, so there are going to be all kinds of people interested in this case. I'll need you to move really quickly on this one, Gorewa," his DPO said.

Gorewa saluted again and walked outside to find an okada taxi to take him to the refugee camp. He would have to pay with his own money and then fill out paperwork for reimbursement, which would take months of snaking through the system before he got it. Still, he was excited. He was always excited at the news of a homicide. He liked to get to the bottom of things, and he would get to the bottom of this one.

The refugee camp used to be a government-owned dairy and corn farm from the colonial days. At some point the dairy farm closed and the corn farm soon became overgrown with grass. The mechanical equipment could be found peeking out of the wild grass. Yet the workers still went and received their salaries at the end of the month. They came in the morning, congregated under a tree where they ate rice and noodles and smoked cigarettes, and then they went home.

When war broke out in Liberia, the government, in desperate search for a place to house the fleeing refugees, suddenly remembered the old farmyard and sent the refugees to live there. They had tried their best to make it into a little Liberia. They played Liberian music, and had little shacks that sold Liberian foods. Some of them left the camp for the day to work in the city and came back at night—mostly women and a few tired old men and children. It was to this camp that the man who we met earlier drinking a bottle of 33 Export arrived one evening, holding a black walking stick. No sooner had he arrived than he made his importance known: he was no ordinary refugee; he was the personal assistant to a warlord. He claimed that the walking stick he carried at all times was no ordinary stick, but was made out of diamonds. It had once belonged to Samuel Doe, but the warlord who was his boss had confiscated it when Doe was captured. He was keeping the diamond walking stick safe for the warlord, who was still fighting in Liberia.

This was an impressive thing; an amazing story. No one in the camp had that kind of closeness to warlords, power, and diamonds. The man who drank 33 Export became the most respected man there.

Sergeant Gorewa went immediately to the chairman of the camp. He knew the chairman from a couple of months back when he was investigating the sale of marijuana. When they had talked, the chairman had convinced him that this was no big deal and that he was in charge of the camp.

The chairman took Sergeant Gorewa to the small shack where the dead man had lived and died. It was constructed from rusted roofing sheets. The stiff body lay in one corner, where it was attracting flies in large numbers because of the small space and the heat. There was a deep stab wound on the neck. Whoever had stabbed the man knew how to wield a knife. No man could survive that kind of wound, Gorewa mused.

The chairman disclosed that the only thing taken from the room was the black walking stick.

"What black walking stick?" Sergeant Gorewa asked.

"The man always had a black walking stick with him," the chairman explained. "He said he used to be the next-in-command and personal assistant to one of the warlords, and that the walking stick was made from diamonds. He was holding onto it for his boss, and when he received the order he would sell the diamonds and be rich."

"Was the stick actually made of diamonds?" Gorewa inquired.

"Between you and me and my God, I do not know whether he was telling the truth. But he sure used that stick to get the girls, and he always had money to drink. You should go ask the woman who runs the bar over there—she might have more answers than I do. He spent practically all his days there."

The woman who owned the bar was dark, plump, and talkative. She said the dead man was a great customer and had a sweet tongue. She gestured to a lizard on the rusted roof of the bar, saying that the dead man could convince the lizard to get off the roof, come sit at the table, and buy him a bottle of 33 Export. She added that he was also a great debtor, and brought out a blue ledger to show Sergeant Gorewa how much the dead man owed.

"What about the walking stick?" Gorewa prompted.

The woman replied that everyone in the camp knew about the walking stick; that the trouble was that the man had gone to a bar in Agege and had boasted about it. This had probably fallen on the ears of the wrong people, and they had come to the camp, stabbed the man to death, and made away with the walking stick.

"Did you believe that it was made of diamonds?"

She said that it was hard to be a refugee, and that the war had brought out the worst in some Liberians. She really wanted to believe that the walking stick was made of diamonds. This was the version of things she preferred; it was a good story. The idea of a stick made of diamonds was something that brightened her dark life as a refugee in a bewildering country.

Sergeant Gorewa's mind began to work on many things at once, the way it always did. It was going to be easy to find out who committed the crime. He would go to his friend Alhaji, who bought gold and diamonds at Agege Market and ask him to be on the lookout for a diamond walking stick. It was bound to turn up sooner rather than later, and he would make the arrest quickly.

Yet something troubled Sergeant Gorewa. In fact, many things troubled him. How could a man escape the bullets from the war in his own country only to be killed by a knife in a strange land? Next, he recalled something that the woman had said about the dead man—that he had a big mouth. She had then elaborated to suggest that the dead man was a boastful person, and added that it was the guy's mouth that got him killed. He wondered about the woman's choice of words too: the man had been killed by a knife, from another man's hand, and yet his mouth must share the blame for his death.

Sergeant Gorewa also wondered if he really wanted to find out if the man had been telling the truth about his walking stick. His instinct told him that the man had been lying, but he really loved the idea of a walking stick made out of diamonds.

The schoolchildren looked out for the man drinking beer and dancing for a couple of days, but he did not appear. They did not miss him; it was no big loss. They had many other games to occupy their time. They walked, ran, and kicked up sand. They picked up stones and decided they were going to throw them at the agama lizards.

UNCLE SAM

BY LEYE ADENLE

Murtala Muhammed International Airport

Dougal was hot and he was afraid. He had been warned about this, the heat. He'd shrugged it off at the time. Everybody knows Africa is hot. It is Africa, after all. But when he stepped out of the British Airways jet and onto the ramp and he inhaled the hot air, it felt like he was drowning standing up. He was instantly wet under the armpits and around the neck. He wished to sweet Jesus he could just take off the white jacket. Heck, other than a couple of men in suits—and they were black—he was the only one not dressed for the tropics. Underneath, his Marks & Spencer cotton shirt was already showing patches of sweat.

It was not too late; he could take off the darn jacket. A patch of blue had blossomed out from the bottom of the chest pocket. Sudoku. He had forgotten to replace the cap when he'd folded the complimentary copy of the *Guardian* away and put the ballpoint pen into the pocket. Then he'd made it worse when he asked the stewardess for water. He had dipped the surprisingly large and thick napkin from the meal pack in water and tried to dab the ink away. The stain taunted his OCD. It was cruel that he had to keep the jacket on.

He could turn back and refuse to leave the aircraft, but instead he continued walking along the dusty blue carpet of the ramp, Nigerians brushing past him with their bulging hand luggage and their unapologetic impatience.

He had never been to Africa. Nigeria seemed the wrong place to start. He followed occasional signs and the throng that had overtaken him, and eventually arrived at the immigration booths where he was told by a man not in uniform to join a different queue. The foreign passports queue. And it was just as long as the impossibly long one he'd been on. There couldn't have been this many people on the flight. Thirty sweltering minutes later, he walked through baggage claim and out into the arrivals lounge of Murtala Muhammed International Airport. He was truly in Lagos. What the hell was he doing?

He stayed in the lounge, surrounded by Nigerians who paid him no notice and men and women in different uniforms—some armed, some not—and he looked out of the floor-to-ceiling glass panes at the waiting crowd staring back into the lounge. He could see the heat outside rising off the top of cars that pulled up to collect passengers. Still, it was not too late.

It was eight in the morning but he was sweating like he was in a sauna. It felt like he was the only one suffering in the choking heat. The other passengers from his flight seemed fine, naturally. He found a tall, free-standing air-conditioning unit whirling out air from dirty vents and stood in front of it. He watched the vents with suspicion. He imagined he could smell the dust. He even tasted it in the back of his throat. Or it could just be the smell of Lagos itself. A police officer was seated on a stool next to the refrigerator-sized machine, the barrel of a Kalashnikov resting on his crotch, his head bent to a noisy game he was playing on his phone. He had no epaulets on his shoulders. He could be any rank in any force.

"Do you need a taxi, sir?"

Dougal swung around. A girl with a brown face that glistened as much as her glossy red lipstick was standing next to him. He shook his head. She didn't leave; she just stood there staring at him. He looked outside, conscious of where she stood and where his bag lay on the ground.

In the sun, amongst the crowd of people on the other side of the road, a man was holding up a large card with his name written on it: *Dougal McManaman*. It wasn't too late. Yet.

"We have air-conditioned cars for hire," the girl said.

"No thanks, I'm fine."

By the time Dougal peered back out the window, the card with his name on it was gone and a mosaic of brown faces, each of them looking the same as any other, stared his way. He panicked. Then the card went up again. The man holding it up had only taken a second to mop sweat from his forehead. Dougal did the same with the sleeve of his white jacket and saw the blue ink stain on the pocket as he did so. He just wished he could take the darn thing off. He was cooking under it. The stain was testing the limits of his self-restraint. He looked at it again, even though he didn't want to, and again it made his skin crawl.

The man outside did not look like a chief. He couldn't be Chief Ernest Abraham Okonkwo II, who spoke with an American accent, invited Dougal to Nigeria, paid for the first-class ticket, and reserved the presidential suite at the Sheraton Hotel. This new man was young, glancing about constantly—like he was on the lookout—and was wearing a brown costume that was faded at the shoulders.

Dougal tried again for a signal on his phone. He'd had no luck when the jet was on the runway. The mobile still had his UK SIM card. The network had assured him his roaming had been sorted. He did stress, several times, that he was traveling to Nigeria. Maybe he'd upset the customer support lad. Maybe the Indian chap in some call center in Bangalore was punishing him. He switched the phone off and on as Betsy always did when she thought something was wrong with her own phone. Around him, other people were using their phones. Phones worked in Nigeria. He held the phone up—nothing.

Betsy had warned him not to come. She told him to call the police. She went on the Internet and printed out dozens of stories about Nigerian fraudsters—419, they call them. But Dougal had shared the news with Matthew, Betsy's brother, who had been the best man at their wedding. Matthew had looked up Okonkwo & Associates and the lawyer's website seemed legit. They were even on Wikipedia. Matthew showed all these to Betsy, but she said she knew Dougal would be kidnapped.

Okonkwo, who had strangely insisted on being called Chief Ernest, promised to be at the airport in Lagos. The chief swore by his mother that he would route his private jet via Lagos first thing in the morning, before leaving for Monaco, so he could be there when the plane from England arrived. But it wasn't the chief holding up the name card now, it couldn't be. And there was no way to contact him to ask if it was safe to go with this stranger outside.

"Are you waiting for a taxi?"

Dougal had been aware of the man who'd come to stand next to him in front of the hopeless air conditioner. He'd even shifted a little to the side so the man could also get some dusty, coolish air. The slender, bespectacled man had placed his briefcase on the floor between them. Dougal remembered him from the flight. They had shared the first-class cabin with just two other passengers: a black girl who looked too young to be traveling alone, and a slightly stooped white man who wore a dark suit and kept asking for more champagne. He was also standing by the glass pane now, the stooped white man, within earshot, looking out for his driver, perhaps, or maybe he was a sheep, instinctively sticking close to the one person who looked like him. They were about the same height. One could even say they looked alike. Somewhat.

"Are you waiting to be picked up?" the black man asked.

"I think that lad there is mine," Dougal said. He pointed at the man with the name card. The stooped man seemed to be listening.

"I see. Erm, listen, I couldn't help overhearing your conversation on the flight. Before we took off. You were talking to someone on the phone."

"Yes." Dougal took a more careful look at the man. On the aircraft, he had been reading a copy of the *Financial Times* before he pulled out a computer and worked on what looked like spreadsheets. He had also declined the champagne and didn't have any alcohol with his meal—unlike the stooped man who couldn't have enough of the stuff.

"Again, I must apologize," the black man said, "but from what I heard, it sounds like you are being swindled."

"What do you mean?"

The man looked at the officer, whose head was bent to his phone. "Someone you've never met invited you to do some business with him, yes?"

He was taller than Dougal, who took a step back and took him all in.

The man continued, "They paid for your flight, booked you a hotel, and maybe even sent you some money?"

Dougal nodded. "They sent money; Western Union."

The man smiled and shook his head. "And this business, whatever it is, you stand to make a lot of money from it, yes?"

Dougal nodded.

"Without spending a lot of your own money?"

Dougal stared at him.

"Or none of your own money," the man went on.

Dougal searched his pockets for his cigarettes.

"If you don't mind me asking, what is this business? They told you they are in possession of some millions of pounds and they need an account to keep it in?" He searched Dougal's face. "They said they are related to a former head of state and they need to get his assets out of the country?"

Dougal looked outside, at the man holding up his name.

"They said you inherited some millions from a relative who died in Nigeria?"

"Yes, my uncle. He moved to Nigeria in the sixties. He married a Nigerian woman."

The man chuckled. "And he left you a lot of millions, right?"

"They said they'd been looking for me for some time."

The man bent over with laughter and gripped Dougal's arm as if to stop himself from hitting the ground. A gold Rolex peeped out from under his sleeve. His grip was tight.

Dougal thought of Betsy. He still had the five thousand pounds, anyway. He would take her on holiday to Mabaya. That would sort her. "What should I do?"

With the back of his hand, the man cleaned tears from his eyes. "Dugal, right?"

Dougal pronounced his name properly for him.

"See, the only reason I came to talk to you is because I saw you standing here, having second thoughts, I assume. Let me ask you something—are you a rich man?"

"No, I'm a schoolteacher."

"What about this uncle of yours, was he rich?"

Dougal shook his head. "He ran a bar."

The man tried, but couldn't talk and laugh at the same

time, so he turned his face from Dougal and bent over laughing again, holding his belly with both his arms. Dougal looked around. A few people glanced at them. The policeman looked up briefly and then continued with his game.

"My friend, there is no money and no Uncle Sam," the man said after he managed to straighten back up. "It was probably a lucky guess that you happened to have a relative in Nigeria. Did you even know the man?"

"No."

"And they know you are not rich?"

"What?"

"The people who invited you. They know you are a schoolteacher, yes?"

"Yes."

"Do they know what you look like?"

"No. They asked me to wear this." Dougal held his arms out. His eyes went to the blue stain.

"A white suit is strange in Nigeria."

"Yes."

"So they don't know what you look like. Thank God for that."

"Why? What are you getting at, anyway? Who are you?"

"I will tell you who I am in a minute. First, like I said, I got suspicious when I overheard your conversation on the plane. You see that man out there? He is here to kidnap you."

A loud gong went off in Dougal's head. He looked at the man outside and his body felt weak from the furious beating of his heart. Betsy was right. It felt as if she was standing next to him, rebuking, mocking him with her silence. Her unspoken *I told you so* permanently etching itself into one of the wrinkles under her eyes. What a fool he'd been. But they sent him money. He still had some of it. They sent him money, and they knew his uncle. They even knew he was his mother's half brother from her first marriage to an Irish miner. How could they know all those things? He'd asked, just to be sure, and after a couple of days, Okonkwo—Chief Earnest—called and said the tattoo was of a bird in flight. A dove on the departed relative's shoulder. How could they have found that out if they didn't know the man? They could have dug up his grave. He shuddered. But who would go to that extent just to lure a schoolteacher to Lagos to be kidnapped? Who would they demand ransom from? Betsy?

"They're going to kidnap me?"

"Yes. He will kidnap you and your family will pay them ransom to release you."

"But . . ."

"But what? You people make me angry. You have never been to Nigeria, maybe you don't even know any Nigerians, and some stranger calls you and says come to Nigeria to collect some millions you didn't work for, and you come. Next thing, you get kidnapped and they'll be saying Nigerians are bad, Nigerians are this, Nigerians are that. I have a mind to arrest you for conspiracy to defame Nigeria."

"What?"

The man reached into his breast pocket and pulled out an ID card. He held it up to Dougal's face. "I am a director of the anticorruption agency here."

The police officer hopped from his stool and stood to attention. His phone sang away in his clenched fist as his eyes darted back and forth between the men standing before him.

Dougal could see it now: Betsy receiving the call. They would put him on to let her know it was no joke, then they'd warn her not to call the police. She would tell them how they had no money. They would tell her to sell the house or take a loan on it. They'd probably already planned everything. The money they sent, the cost of the flight, it was all just an investment. Betsy would take out the loan, she wouldn't call the police, and the kidnappers would get their money. It was all so sophisticated.

"What should I do?" Dougal asked.

"What do I care? Just don't get yourself kidnapped in my country."

Dougal felt stupid. He stared at the man whose countenance had gone from unrestrained bemusement to pure disgust. Dougal was desperate for help. His face pleaded on his behalf.

"Look," the man said, "get rid of that jacket, for one."

Dougal looked down at himself, his eyes drawn to the stain. It was ruined, anyway. He hurriedly took off the jacket. His shirt was wet and clung to his body. He folded the jacket then unfolded it and rolled it up.

"Get rid of it," the man said.

Dougal understood. The jacket was like a target painted onto him. He glanced around for where to stash the cheap thing.

The man held out his hand. "Give it to me," he said.

Dougal handed over the jacket. "What now?" he asked.

The man picked up his bag and in an unnecessarily loud voice said, "You are what they call *mumu* over here. If you are lucky, you'll get a flight back to England today. If you step out there, be ready to lose everything you ever worked for in your life. And maybe even your life itself."

Dougal watched him go, then peered at the man outside, then locked eyes with the police officer who was still standing rigid and appearing confused, then looked back at the man who had saved him from being kidnapped. He turned around to check for the stooped white man from the flight, for safety. He was gone.

Dougal picked up his bag from the ground. At least he hadn't lost any money, and he still had theirs. He had come out tops. Yes, he'd taken time to off fly to Nigeria during term time, he'd lost two days of holiday for that, but he still had their money. If only he could get out of Nigeria before they found him. Before they figured out that he'd been warned. He imagined the chap waiting outside bursting into the airport and chasing him down. His heart beat even faster.

At the British Airways desk, Dougal asked the lady if he could use his return ticket to get on the next available flight home.

The lady took the ticket from him and inspected it. "Sir, you just arrived this morning."

"I just want to get the hell out of this place," Dougal muttered.

Betsy would agree with him that they had made a profit out of the failed kidnap attempt. If she would go along with him and leave out the flight to Nigeria, he could tell the story to their friends about how he had outsmarted Nigerian con artists. If she played along and they both pretended he never actually took the flight.

The woman shifted backward in her chair and called over to a male colleague.

Matthew would play along. After all, he'd also fallen for the con. It was as much his fault that Dougal had almost gotten kidnapped in Lagos. He shivered. It'd been so close. If not for the eavesdropping gentleman from the flight. So close. But the bastards had done their homework well; the only thing that still puzzled him was why they chose a poor schoolteacher—of all the *mumus* in London, why him? And how on earth did they get to know so much about Uncle Sam?

"Sir, what seems to be the problem?" the male attendent asked. "Sir? Sir? Sir, is everything okay? Sir?"

"How did he know his name?" Dougal said, staring into the man's face.

"What, sir?"

"The man, the anticorruption man, how did he know my uncle is called Sam? I never told him my uncle's name. How did he know it?"

"What are you talking about, sir?"

"He knew my uncle's name. How could he have known that, unless . . . Oh my God. I've been swindled. He's the con!"

"Are you waiting for Dougal?"

The driver checked the name written on the name card and nodded, even though what the man said didn't sound like what he read. And he was there to pick up a white man, not a Nigerian like the slender, bespectacled man in a suit standing in front of him. But next to the Nigerian was a white man, slightly stooped, mopping his forehead with a damp white handkerchief, and sweating as if water had been poured over his head. And he was wearing a white jacket. The jacket had a large blue stain on its pocket.

KILLER APE

BY CHRIS ABANI

Ikoyi

It was hard to believe that the monkey had done it. Not *monkey*, Okoro thought to himself, crossing the word out in his notebook. He wrote *ape*, and next to it, *chimpanzee*. Accuracy in recoding data and attention to detail were a detective's best friend, especially in a case as bizarre as this one.

"Why would an ape, your pet ape, kill your husband?" Okoro asked the white woman who was standing by the French doors holding the midsized ape like a baby. It clung to her, and an expression of sorrow in its eyes made it look vulnerable. The terry cloth diaper it was wearing exacerbated this and made it appear even more like a baby. That look belied the blood on its hands, thick and even, matting the fur. The chimpanzee had clearly tried to lick its hands clean and had left blood all around its mouth. It was an unsettling sight, although Okoro wasn't sure if it was more the idea of a murdering chimpanzee or the fact that this was a pet wearing diapers. The British in Nigeria were a strange bunch, he thought. This woman, he thought, glancing at his notes, this Dorothy Parker, was particularly strange.

The light coming in through the French doors was dusty and mote-laden. It spilled across the expensive Berber rug, falling on the body of Gordon Parker. He was lying facedown in a pool of his own blood. There were several nasty cuts on the back of his head, and a large bump had risen.

Mrs. Dorothy Parker blew a long stream of smoke out of the French doors from the cigarette she was smoking. Pinched between forefinger and thumb, it was in an ivory holder with a gold inlay, an expensive piece. There was a deliberateness to her that made Okoro think that she was very likely not the emotional kind.

"How would I know?" Dorothy Parker responded. "Bobo here has many gifts, but speech is not one of them."

At the mention of its name, the chimpanzee paused in licking its hands and peered at the woman. They made eye contact and the ape lowered its gaze as though afraid of what it saw in hers.

Okoro noted this and wondered if it was a frame job. But the idea was so absurd he was at a loss to explain how or why anyone would frame a chimpanzee for murder. He thought about asking her, but instead said: "Bobo? That's not the name I expected you to have given him, Mrs. Parker. There is something about you that makes me think you'd have chosen a name like Theodore."

Dorothy Parker looked Okoro up and down and snorted. He couldn't tell if she was expressing amusement or derision.

"Theodore? Why that would have been perfect, but my husband loved the circus. He did have an unnatural affinity for the lower classes," she said.

"How do you mean, Mrs. Parker?" Okoro asked.

"Oh, I don't know. He had cheap tastes. Liked to hang out with the natives more than us expatriates. I mean, no offense, Sergeant . . ."

"Okoro," Okoro said.

"Yes, quite," Dorothy Parker replied. "As I said, no offense, but our sort of people have little in common with the likes of the natives."

"I see your point. Keeping an ape as a child must be much more preferable to mingling with us lowly humans," Okoro said.

Dorothy Parker flushed from embarrassment but said nothing.

Detective Sergeant Okoro had caught the weekend shift, which he typically didn't mind because it was an easy one. Much of the work happened on Saturday nights, the usual run-of-the-mill fights and stabbings and then the occasional murder, but a light load. Lately, most people in Lagos were dying in robber-related crimes, which often meant that to avoid turf wars, Homicide detectives gave up those cases to Robbery. When Okoro suggested the two units be merged into one, Robbery/Homicide, he was met with derision and dismissal. Stabbing-related deaths mostly occurred in the clubs and brothels which again involved ceding many cases to Vice. This was why Homicide's caseload was quite light, something all the veterans in the unit seemed to love, and they would fight anything that changed the status quo. Anyway, there were few detectives in the Homicide unit who liked or knew how to execute proper forensic investigations.

Even the white British Scotland Yard–trained detectives who worked alongside the Nigerians knew little of the forensic methods that fascinated Okoro. The fact that he drew most of his "technical" knowledge from the fictional Sherlock Holmes did little to help his credibility. Though he was a detective sergeant, Okoro had very little power, and he found himself overruled even by junior white colleagues with whom the beat commanders always sided. He knew his promotion was more about the British trying to prepare an officer corps to hand over power to than about any real change or an actual belief in the Nigerian officer's abilities. This meant Okoro had to toe the line unless he wasn't assigned his own single-officer cases. Toeing the line meant going out on calls, taking witness statements, and then returning to file reports, which placed the blame for the crime on the individual the investigating officers intuited might be guilty, followed by a confession that was beaten out of them as efficiently and quickly as possible to close cases.

That meant Sundays for Okoro were usually a slow day of report-writing at the station. But this morning a call had come in, from Ikoyi, which in itself was a surprise given that the wealthy suburb had very few crimes, much less murders. Okoro was the only detective on duty, which automatically made this case a single-officer investigation, and for him meant that he could channel as much Sherlock Holmes as possible. To say he was excited was to understate matters. Maybe closing this case using his preferred methods was just what he needed to earn him the credibility he so desperately needed.

It was bad enough that his manner of dress—clean shirts, pressed suits, polished wingtips, and the occasional fedora—in a unit where his colleagues looked like they had just rolled out of a brothel and straight into work, earned him the taunts of *dandy*. A euphuism he knew really meant homosexual. He rationalized it away by putting the bullying down to the manner of the men in these kinds of jobs. He rarely challenged them for fear of confirming their suspicions about him. It would be dangerous for him on many levels if anyone knew he liked men. There was the anti-sodomy law which had been used in the mother country to imprison one of his heroes, Oscar Wilde. It was still on the law books here in the colony and would be enforced with no difficulty. Then there was his career, which he couldn't afford to have derailed. Men like him knew how to keep quiet, how to spot in silence the codes that revealed like-minded men, sympathetic men. Theirs was a lifestyle conducted in subterfuge, the secrets and ways of it closely guarded.

Detective James Okoro loved motorcycles. If he could afford one he would have liked an original 1950 Indian Chief, but he could only afford a 1949 Vespa 125 Corsa, with an aluminum alloy frame. It looked quite nice and its high-pitched engine whine sounded to him like a siren and he loved that he could turn heads. As he rode across the mainland bridge toward Ikoyi, he felt his excitement growing

It was a quiet Lagos Sunday and the rich residential area of lkoyi was lush with green palms, manicured lawns, and shocks of red hibiscus, purple bougainvillea, and yellow sunflowers. It was 1958 and the eve of independence. The air of freedom, of hope, was palpable. Already this once all-white neighborhood was a salt-and-pepper mix. The elite Nigerians, prepping for their takeover of power, had already moved in. Actually, it probably wasn't accurate to say that it was once an all-white locale because even in the late nineteenth century there were rich locals living here, and Detective Sergeant Okoro was particular about accuracy. That was what made Sherlock Holmes such a success. Attention to detail.

Unlike most of the other houses on the street, this one had no gate or fence. Just thick ivy shrubs for privacy and a gravel-filled driveway with a black Morris Minor parked at the end of it. Okoro took in the well-kept grounds and noted that there was probably a gardener on staff, should that be relevant. He came to heavy double front doors, the wood carved elaborately with local motifs and scenes. It was beautiful and made Okoro wish he could own a place with doors like that.

He pulled the rope hanging from the door, weighted by the brass figure of an Oba of Benin. Deep inside the house he heard the chime of an old bell.

A man appeared at the door. He was in his late thirties. Handsome and very dark, he wore a beige khaki uniform—a starched safari jacket and shorts—and his feet were laced into very shiny oxblood oxford shoes. "Are you the policeman?" he asked.

Okoro surmised he must be the houseboy. He never understood that term. It could only be meant to demean, as most houseboys were usually above thirty and more like butlers in the range of the work they did and in their ability to run households. They were often very well spoken and educated. Some of them had a few other houseboys and maids working under them. They were like fathers to these young men and women, and many used their position and privilege to educate their wards who might otherwise never have that opportunity. Okoro respected them.

"Yes, and you must be Mr. . . . ?"

"Good morning, sir. I'm not mister, just Emmanuel. My name is Emmanuel."

"Well, good morning, Emmanuel. Am I at the right place? I hear there has been a murder?"

Emmanuel looked Okoro over. Both men seemed to recognize something about the other, but when Okoro leaned in to take a better look, Emmanuel glanced away, behind Okoro, as though searching for more policemen.

"Are you alone, sir?" the houseboy asked.

The moment had been fleeting, and Okoro couldn't be sure, so he let it go.

"Yes, I am. No need for a lot of officers to investigate a death."

Okoro noticed something in Emmanuel's eyes at the word *death*. A reddening of the eyes, a wetness, and then a quick shift of the gaze away. He knew from the call that had come in that morning that the person who had died was Emmanuel's boss. Okoro was surprised that an employer's death would elicit this kind of response from the houseboy.

"Is everything all right?" Okoro asked.

"Of course, sir. This way, please," Emmanuel replied.

He led Okoro down a wide hallway with hard ceramic floor tiles that rang out underfoot. There were big-framed black-and-white photos on the walls. In every photograph, there was an ape alone, or an ape being held by a woman. There was only one image of a couple on their wedding day.

"No children?" Okoro asked Emmanuel.

"No sir, just the monkey."

"And do you have any idea who might have killed your master?"

"Madam says the monkey killed Gordon," Emmanuel responded.

"Gordon? You called your master by his first name?"

"Mr. Parker, I m-meant to say," Emmanuel stammered.

"But you said Gordon. That means something."

"It's just a mistake, sir. We are mourning the loss here."

Okoro smiled at Emmanuel's discomfort. He knew there was more. It was not uncommon for white bosses to take up affairs with staff—usually female though. Maybe it was nothing. There was enough going on here and he couldn't afford to be distracted. Sherlock Holmes wouldn't approve. It was the easiest way to miss the small details that can break a case wide open.

"It is a chimpanzee, I can see that from the photos," Okoro said. "So, it's an ape, not a monkey."

Emmanuel nodded and began to walk again. "Yes sir," he said. "The monkey is an ape. This way, please."

Emmanuel led Okoro into a large living room at the end of the hall. It was airy and full of light from the French doors at the far end that led into the garden. Emmanuel stopped at the entrance to the living room, refusing to go inside. He glanced briefly at the body on the floor and looked away. A woman stood by the French doors holding a chimpanzee in a diaper in her arms.

"Madam, this is the police," Emmanuel announced, and turned to leave.

Okoro stepped forward. "Good morning, Mrs. Parker. I am Detective Sergeant Okoro."

Okoro moved around the crime scene, viewing it from different angles, searching for a clue. For anything that might reveal what had happened there. There was something in the way that the body was lying, spread-eagle. Clearly the body had fallen forward and it was also clear that the blow had been delivered from behind and that it had caught the victim unawares. But the knees were all wrong, as if the victim had been kneeling when struck. But that made no sense—why would a man be kneeling in his living room? Perhaps he had been made to kneel, which suggested a premeditated murder, an execution even. That would rule out the chimpanzee. It wasn't that Okoro had any difficulty believing a chimpanzee would kill a man. They were in fact killers, and carnivorous too. They ate their young sometimes and definitely ate other monkeys. But they only attacked if they felt threatened. What would make a pet feel threatened?

"Did your husband get along with Bobo?"

"Yes, Gordon doted on him. Why? This wasn't Gordon's

fault," she said, and paused. "Or Bobo's, for that matter. Just a dreadful accident."

"Of course," Okoro muttered. His gaze drifted back to the body. Something was off. He bent down and examined the wound on Gordon's head. The whole back of his head had been ravaged. No teeth marks, no claw marks. The beating had been savage though it looked like it had been done by a manmade object. Something metal perhaps.

"Are there any objects missing from this room, Mrs. Parker?"

"I don't know. Ask Emmanuel, that's his job."

Okoro nodded. "Emmanuel," he called out.

Emmanuel appeared at the door as if by magic. Okoro thought it strange he hadn't heard him clacking up on the tile flooring.

"Yes sir," Emmanuel said. He stood at the door, seemingly reluctant to enter the living room. His eyes seemed glued to Gordon's body. And there was that look on his face again. A deep sorrow and grief. Why? Okoro wondered to himself.

"Are there any objects missing from this room, Emmanuel?"

"I don't steal," Emmanuel replied, his voice soft in tone but with an edge as sharp as a knife. He locked eyes on Mrs. Parker—the look between them was chilling. Okoro missed none of it.

"I'm sorry, Emmanuel," Okoro said, breaking the tension. "I didn't mean to imply that. I am curious about what might have been the murder weapon."

The houseboy pointed at the chimpanzee, or maybe Mrs. Parker. "That's the murder weapon," he said.

Okoro nodded. He prowled around the living room, looking for a sign of anything displaced, any dust rings left behind after something heavy and metal had been moved. He couldn't find anything.

"What is going on here, sergeant, what exactly are you implying?" Dorothy Parker asked.

"I'm not implying anything. Just doing my job."

"I've told you what happened. Bobo here had an incident, and killed my poor Gordon."

"Of course, Mrs. Parker. Remind me again how you know for sure Bobo killed your husband? Were you a witness?"

"I didn't see it happen but when I came into the room when Gordon wasn't answering my calls, I saw Bobo standing over him covered in blood."

"Standing over him? Like he had just clobbered him to death?"

"Yes, like that."

"Was anyone else in the room?" Turning rapidly to Emmanuel before Dorothy Parker could answer, Okoro said: "And you, Emmanuel. Where were you when it happened?"

The man seemed lost in a daze.

"How long did you work for Mr. Parker?" Okoro asked him.

"Too long, really, wouldn't you say?" Dorothy Parker answered for him.

Emmanuel blinked but said nothing.

Okoro turned to Dorothy Parker. "Was he a religious man, your husband?"

"No, not at all religious. Why do you ask?"

"Something about the way the body is lying."

"The body? That's my husband!"

"Of course, madam. My apologies. There is something about the way your husband is lying that suggests he was kneeling when he was struck."

"You can tell that from the way he's lying?"

"Yes. Is there any other reason your husband may have been kneeling?"

Dorothy Parker flushed at the question and Emmanuel swallowed and looked away quickly.

"Prayer?" she said, more question than answer.

"But you just said he wasn't at all religious."

"Mr. Parker found religion tiresome," Emmanuel interjected.

Okoro and Dorothy Parker both turned to look at him.

"I'm sorry," Emmanuel mumbled. "I had no right."

Dorothy Parker cut her eyes at him, then turned to Okoro. "Gordon wasn't much of anything, really. Just a civil servant."

Okoro studied her for a minute. She seemed way too collected and calm for a woman who'd found her husband dead in their house just that morning. But she was white and English and he had heard they were cold; *emotionally stunted*, his father had called them. He would know, he had fought alongside them in Burma in the Second World War.

Okoro took out a small camera and began taking pictures.

"Why are you taking photographs?" Dorothy Parker asked.

"The latest in criminal investigation, madam. We preserve the scene for posterity. Even here in the colonies we like to keep up with the latest. Did I tell you Sherlock Holmes, the great British detective, is a hero of mine?"

"Why and when would you have told me that? Also, you do know that he isn't real, don't you?"

"Real enough for Scotland Yard to learn from."

"Look, I don't want to be rude, but as you can imagine, this has been an overwhelming day. When can I expect you to be done?"

"When I am done, madam—I'll be gone when I'm done. Have you had a good strong cup of tea? I hear you English find it helps with shock. I'm more of a Scottish man myself."

"Do you mean a Scotch man?"

Okoro smiled. "Something like that."

"You are quite rude," Dorothy Parker said. "I shall be making a report to your superiors."

"Of course, that is your right, madam. I would expect nothing less." As Okoro took the photographs, he mentally ran through the questions he hadn't asked. What would Sherlock do? He paused and looked up. "Can Emmanuel hold Bobo for a moment?"

"I don't want to hold the monkey, sir," Emmanuel said. "I don't like dirty animals."

"You would know," Dorothy Parker spat.

This exchange confirmed in Okoro's mind what he had already suspected—Gordon Parker had been involved in an affair with his houseboy. And the wife knew. Yet the thing between her and Emmanuel, the subdued and seething rage, smelled of some kind of collusion, but a forced one. Okoro turned his attention once more to Mrs. Dorothy Parker.

"Can you put Bobo down?" he asked.

"Why? You bloody—"

"I wouldn't recommend finishing that statement Mrs. Parker," Okoro cut her off. "I need to examine your hands and take photos."

Dorothy Parker reluctantly set Bobo down. Okoro watched as the ape ambled over to Gordon's body. It stopped just short of it and began to whimper, rocking from side to side. It dipped its hands in the blood on the floor, which was now congealed, and held them up in what looked like awe. It kept whimpering. There was a look of sadness and something else in Dorothy Parker's face. The first crack in her façade that he had seen. She held out her hands. Okoro reached for them and she pulled back. He smiled and lifted his camera instead and resumed taking photos. There were strange cuts on her hands.

"How did you get those marks?" Okoro asked her.

"Bobo gave them to me."

"Don't look like claw marks," he said. "Looks like something sharp nicked you a few times."

She said nothing.

"How long was your husband dead before you called?"

"I called as soon as I found him," she said.

Okoro nodded, then asked to see Emmanuel's hands. The houseboy held them out. Not a mark on them. No callus or blister, not even a scratch, and they were soft to the touch. He clearly didn't do any of the strenuous work around here.

"Are there other servants that work here?"

"Yes sir," Emmanuel said.

"Take me to them." Turning to Dorothy Parker, who was now holding Bobo again, the blood from his paws all over her blouse, Okoro said: "As soon as I have interviewed the rest of the staff, I will be pretty much done here. In the meantime, I do have to call the coroner's office to come and take your husband. May I use your telephone?"

Dorothy Parker waved at the phone on a side table.

Okoro dialed the number and spoke softly into the receiver, then turned back to Dorothy Parker. "Thank you, madam. Please excuse me."

Emmanuel led him out of the room, through the kitchen, and across the garden to the servants' quarters. As they walked Okoro turned to Emmanuel. Best to confront this head on, that's how Sherlock would have handled it. A confession can be extracted without a beating, Okoro told himself.

"I think you know how your boss died," he said. "What's more, I think you were there when it happened."

"I really don't know what you're talking about," Emmanuel responded, not breaking his stride.

"How long were you having sex with Gordon Parker?"

Emmanuel stopped, his shoulders slumping, face down.

"I know. And I know that you know that I know," Okoro said.

"You know nothing," Emmanuel said in a choked whisper.

Okoro put his hand on Emmanuel's shoulder. "Trust me, I know. I know because we are the same. Because I can tell. From your manner, from the faint traces of tiro around your eyes, from the way you looked at him, from the way she reacted to you. I know. Tell me what happened here, Emmanuel."

The houseboy sank to his knees, tears running down his face.

"Confess to me and I will find a way to make it right for you. I know you didn't kill Gordon. I suspect his wife did it. Now, I know you know homosexuality is against the law, but the bigger thing here is murder. No one will care about that if you just tell me what happened, what I need to convict her."

Okoro hated himself for lying. The moment Emmanuel told him what had happened, he would become instrumental as a witness and his homosexuality would emerge. There was no easy way to solve this and protect the innocent. There was love in the way Emmanuel reacted when Gordon's name was mentioned, more than he could say about Dorothy Parker. If anyone was the victim here, it was Emmanuel, and Gordon of course, but he was dead, so that didn't matter so much.

"I don't care about me! I care about him! About him! He is a good man, *was* a good man. If anyone finds out, this will destroy him. I can't let that happen. I can't. I love him."

Emmanuel was crying now, shoulders heaving. The maids and other houseboys had gathered on the veranda of the servants' quarters to watch with sad eyes.

"Go inside!" Okoro commanded them.

They went back inside and shut the door.

Okoro sat next to Emmanuel, facing the opposite direction. "Do you smoke?" he asked, holding out a cigarette.

Emmanuel shook his head.

"Quite right, good man. Filthy habit, really," Okoro said, lighting one up. He smoked half of it next to the sobbing Emmanuel. He could see Dorothy Parker watching them from the French doors of the living room. Finally, he spoke. "So here is what I think happened: You both thought she had gone out and you were about to have sex in the living room. Gordon was on his knees with you in his mouth when she walked in on you. She reacted in shock and anger and hit Gordon in the back of the head with something. Many times, judging by the state of his head. You fled, and while you were gone she hid the murder weapon and called the police and tried to pin this on Bobo . . . Does that sound about right?"

Emmanuel nodded his head. "Except she knew. I think it was an ambush—like she knew," he said between sobs, gulping for breath to force the words out. "She pretended to go out. Took the car. I was making steak, tenderizing the meat, when Gordon called me in. I use the base of a small axe to beat the meat. The same axe I use to cut through bone when I need to. It is very sharp. Anyway, she must have only gone to the end of the road because she was back so soon and surprised us. It all happened so fast."

Okoro patted him on the back. "She used the meat tenderizer?"

"Yes."

Okoro nodded, thinking to himself that this explained both the wounds on Gordon and the cuts on Dorothy Parker's hands. She must have hit Gordon repeatedly with the base of the axe until blood got on the handle, causing it to slip and nick her palms a few times.

"I don't suppose we will ever find the murder weapon?"

"I threw it into the bay," Emmanuel said.

"Of course you did." Okoro thought about how hard all this must have been for Emmanuel. To cooperate with his lover's killer to frame the poor chimpanzee. Could a chimpanzee even be arrested for murder? Charged? What were the laws with regard to animals that attacked and killed their owners? That would be the jurisdiction of Animal Control, not Homicide.

"I love him," Emmanuel said again. "And he loved me too. Why couldn't she let us be? She only loves that monkey, it's unnatural."

Okoro nodded. They sat in the grass for what seemed like a long time while Emmanuel collected himself. Okoro helped him up.

"Can I say goodbye to my wards before you arrest me?" Emmanuel asked.

"For what? You didn't murder Gordon. Besides, what would be gained from all that scandal. It's all quite messy, this whole situation."

"So what happens now?" Emmanuel asked.

"Well, the coroner will be here soon to remove Gordon's body. Say nothing to them. I'm going in to talk to your mistress."

"But . . ."

"But what? The monkey did it. That's what my report will say."

Even Sherlock Holmes would have agreed with him on this decision, of that he was sure. Anyway, he had solved the crime and nobody was beaten to get a confession. In a manner of speaking, he had won. There would be other cases, less complicated in terms of victims and perpetrators, but for now his quiet victory would have to suffice.

Emmanuel remained silent. His eyes said it all.

Okoro headed back inside.

"Well?" Dorothy Parker said. "Are you done here?"

"Yes, I'm done, Mrs. Parker. My verdict is that the monkey did it. May Bobo and Gordon forgive us all."

The last thing Okoro saw was Mrs. Dorothy Parker petting Bobo and whispering soothing sounds. As he walked down the gravel path, the coroner's van pulled up.

"An unusual one, I hear," the coroner said to Okoro.

"Yes, highly irregular," Okoro replied. "Killer ape. That has to be a first."

Back at the station, it was quiet as Detective Sergeant Okoro threaded the report sheet into the typewriter. This was one of those moments when he was grateful there was a line to toe.

ABOUT THE CONTRIBUTORS

Chris Abani

Chris Abani, a Nigerian-born, award-winning poet and novelist, currently teaches at Northwestern University in Chicago. He is the recipient of a PEN USA Freedom-to-Write Award, a Prince Claus Award, a Lannan Literary Fellowship, a California Book Award, a Hurston/Wright Legacy Award, a PEN Beyond Margins Award, a PEN/ Hemingway Award, and a Guggenheim Award.

James Manyika

Leye Adenle is a Nigerian writer whose debut novel, *Easy Motion Tourist*, set in Lagos, won the 2016 Prix Marianne. Leye has also appeared onstage in London in plays including Ola Rotimi's *Our Husband Has Gone Mad Again*. He comes from a family of writers, the most famous of whom was his grandfather, Oba Adeleye Adenle I, a former king of Oshogbo in southwest Nigeria. Leye currently lives in London.

Tolu Talabi

'Pemi Aguda writes short stories, a great number of which have been influenced by the chaotic city of Lagos, where she's lived most of her life. Her short story "Caterer, Caterer" won the 2015 Writivism Short Story Prize.

Femke van Zeijl

A. Igoni Barrett was born in Port Harcourt in 1979 and has lived in Eko (Lagos) since 2007. Most of the stories in his collection *Love Is Power, or Something Like That* were set in the fictional city of Poteko. His first novel, *Blackass*, which was published by Graywolf Press in 2016, was the first time he wrote the city of Lagos into fiction.

Ejiro Onobrakpor

Jude Dibia was born in Lagos, where he spent most of his early years. Lagos has always been an integral part and presence in his writings, from his debut novel *Walking with Shadows*, to his most recent, *Blackbird*. A recipient of the Ken Saro-Wiwa Prize for Prose and a Commonwealth Writing Prize, Dibia continues to work on new fiction from Sweden, where he lives.

Dan Addison

Onyinye Ihezukwu was born in Nigeria, where she worked as a radio broadcaster in Lagos. She is a 2015–2017 Wallace Stegner Fellow at Stanford University.

Wale Lawal

Wale Lawal is a Lagos-based management consultant and the founder/editor of *The Republic: A Journal of Nigerian Affairs*. He tweets from @WalleLawal.

James Manyika

Sarah Ladipo Manyika was raised in Lagos and Jos, Nigeria. She has also lived in Kenya, France, and England. She holds a PhD from the University of California, Berkeley, and currently serves on the boards of Hedgebrook and the Museum of the African Diaspora in San Francisco. Her second novel, *Like a Mule Bringing Ice Cream to the Sun,* was short-listed for the 2016 Goldsmiths Prize.

Pemi Aguda

Uche Okonkwo has an MA in creative writing from the University of Manchester, and has worked as a managing editor at Farafina, a leading Lagos-based independent publisher. Her stories have appeared in *Ploughshares, Per Contra, Ellipsis,* and other outlets, and her 2016 essay "What the Road Offers" was published by Invisible Borders as a limited-edition chapbook. She was a spring 2017 resident at Writers Omi, Ledig House.

Nnedi Okorafor

Nnedi Okorafor is a Nigerian-American writer of speculative fiction and an associate professor at the University at Buffalo, New York. Her works include *Who Fears Death*, the Binti novella series, *The Book of Phoenix*, the Akata Witch series, and *Lagoon*. She is the winner of Hugo, Nebula, and World Fantasy awards and her debut novel *Zahrah the Windseeker* won the prestigious Wole Soyinka Prize for Literature. Learn more about Okorafor at nnedi.com.

E.C. Osondu

E.C. Osondu grew up in Lagos and is the author of the collection of stories *Voice of America* and the novel *This House Is Not For Sale*. He is a winner of the Caine Prize, also known as the "African Booker," and a Pushcart Prize. His fiction has appeared in the *Atlantic*, *AGNI*, *n+1*, *Guernica*, *Kenyon Review*, *McSweeney's*, *New Statesman*, and many other places.

Yitschaq Abia

Adebola Rayo is a full-time writer, editor, and TV series junkie who has lived most of her life in Lagos. Her works have appeared in *234NEXT*, *Saraba Literary Magazine*, and *Sentinel Nigeria*. She has a law degree and no idea what to do with it.

Dilibe Omesub

Chika Unigwe was born and raised in Enugu, Nigeria. Author of several books, including *On Black Sisters' Street* and *Night Dancer*, Unigwe is the 2016 Bonderman Professor of Writing at Brown Uiversity in Providence, Rhode Island.